ROBERT SWINDELLS

# *FOLLOW*
## *—A—*
# *SHADOW*

PUFFIN BOOKS

The author is indebted to
Ms Sally Johnson, Dr Juliet Barker,
Mr David Manley, Ms Dawn Poyner and Ms Brenda Poole
For their help with research.

PUFFIN BOOKS

Published by the Penguin Group
Penguin Books Ltd, 27 Wrights Lane, London W8 5TZ, England
Penguin Books USA Inc., 375 Hudson Street, New York, New York 10014, USA
Penguin Books Australia Ltd, Ringwood, Victoria, Australia
Penguin Books Canada Ltd, 10 Alcorn Avenue, Toronto, Ontario, Canada M4V 3B2
Penguin Books (NZ) Ltd, 182–190 Wairau Road, Auckland 10, New Zealand

Penguin Books Ltd, Registered Offices: Harmondsworth, Middlesex, England

First published by Hamish Hamilton 1989
Published in Penguin Books 1991
Reissued in Puffin Books 1996
3 5 7 9 10 8 6 4 2

Printed in England by Clays Ltd, St Ives plc

*Note*

In the autumn of 1835, when he was eighteen, Branwell Brontë, brother of the famous Brontë sisters went to London with his tutor, Robinson, to seek admittance to the Royal Academy Schools as a student. He returned to Haworth after about a week, and never mentioned the matter again. He had not presented the several letters of introduction he had to influential persons in the capital, and no record exists in Royal Academy archives of his ever having shown his specimen drawings there. He was seen once at a tavern in Holborn called The Castle. Otherwise his movements while in London are unknown.

*For Brenda*

# CONTENTS

# TRICK OF THE LIGHT

Tim's body walked along Petergate with a blank expression on its face. It wasn't much of a body. Five foot three and thin with it. Nothing special about the face, either. Zits. Nose like Concorde. Weak chin. Glasses. A mane of carroty hair. No girls, aching with desire, followed Tim's body as it turned into Cheapside, and if they had he wouldn't have known. He wasn't there.

*

August, 1940. That's where Tim was. Hanging in the straps as his Spitfire rolled off the top of a loop eleven thousand feet above the weald of Kent. The 109 which had been on his tail was now in his gunsight. He smiled tightly into his face-mask as his thumb covered the firing button. The Messerschmitt banked steeply in a desperate bid to shake off its pursuer, but Tim kicked the rudder-pedal, eased the stick over and thumbed the button. Eight Brownings burped. Bits flew off the 109, which flipped on to its back and dived, trailing smoke. Tim followed it down till the pilot baled out; then turned, still smiling, and made for Biggin Hill. 'Tiger' Tim South had made his thirty-ninth kill.

His D.F.C. had just come through when the din of a car horn split his brain and a voice yelled, 'Out the way, you daft little four-eyed gitt!'

*

Tim skipped sideways on to the pavement and walked

1

on, looking sheepish. It's not easy being a six foot hero one second and a daft little four-eyed gitt the next. It's a shock to the system. People were looking at him, with his flaming hair and puny body. He could feel their eyes, the nosy prannocks. He turned a corner to spoil their fun and stood with his hands in his pockets, looking in C & A's window.

Sports gear. A dummy in a jogging suit, frozen in the act of bending to pick up a dumb-bell. Another on an exercise bike. Trainers strewn across the carpet in front of a plastic plant. A card saying 'Slim for Summer'.

That's me, he thought gloomily. Slim for summer. Weedy for winter. Ugly all year round. He was about to move on when he noticed something odd about his reflection in the glass. He was wearing jeans and a teeshirt, whereas his image seemed to be in a dark suit and some sort of weird high collar which came to his chin. His glasses looked different too, though the reflection was too faint for detail. He shifted his stance to get a clearer view but the instant he moved, the illusion was gone. He cupped his hands on the glass and peered in, looking for something which might account for it – a third dummy perhaps – but there was nothing. He shrugged and walked on.

Weird. Like I was dressed up for a play or something. There one second, gone the next, like Tiger Tim the fighter ace. Still, not to worry. Trick of the light, I expect.

# FABULOUS SIGHT

At the turn of the stair – the half-landing on which the old clock stood – I paused, listening. The only sounds I could hear – voices in soft conversation – seemed to come from the kitchen, where one or more of my sisters must be talking with Tabby. My aunt I knew was visiting the sick and my father was busy in the parlour. The afternoon was fine – still and sunny – and the probability was that the others were out walking.

Good. This was the moment I'd waited for. Now I might slip away unseen. So severely was my spirit oppressed that I could not have borne their cheerful salutations, the smiles behind which they habitually conceal their disappointment in me. Eyes soft with love and with pity.

Pity! Who are they to pity me? Am I not a giant – a giant among pygmies? Who in this village can dispute with me and prevail? None. Who can match my intellect? None. My wit? None. And who, of a raw winter's evening before the tavern hearth, is better company? Why nobody, of course. So.

I was about to continue my descent when I became aware of an odd sensation. A sweetish odour assailed my nostrils, and at the same time the objects within my field of vision – the balustrade, the scrubbed woodgrain treads, the pictures on the walls – took on an uncanny sharpness and clarity. It was as though my eyes were focusing properly for the first time, and I felt acutely agitated. The clock's loud ticking seemed to demand my attention. I turned, and gasped at what I saw in the glass.

I saw myself of course, but I have long since trained my eyes not to linger on that ill-favoured image, and it was what lay beyond that made me gasp. It was the city. A place of slender towers which soared glittering to the sky. Glass towers in serried ranks, rank upon rank with straight, clean, tree-lined boulevards between and cloudless skies above. It was perfection. Perfection marred, like all of my visions, by the superimposition upon it of my own stunted likeness.

As I stared, the city set my limbs shaking and then I was falling, falling down the sheer faces of its glittering towers, blinded by the light.

# MORE LIKE YOUR SISTER

Sunday breakfast. Cornflakes, sausages and bacon, toast and marmalade, interrogation. Mum, lips pursed, digging in the Vitalite. Dad with his reading glasses on, looking over the top of the *Sunday Times*.

'What your mother's saying, Tim, is that fifteen's not old enough to start staying out half the night without offering some sort of explanation. She sat up till half past eleven waiting for you. We both did. We were worried. Then when you finally showed up you grunted something we didn't catch, slammed off to your room and put a record on. It must have been one o'clock before either of us got to sleep.'

Tim stared at his plate. That grease-smear's a cloud, right? And that black speck in it looks just like a crippled bomber – a Heinkel – limping home at dawn. Now. If I move the bacon-rind—'

'Tim!'

He looked up. 'What?'

'Are you listening to what I'm saying to you?'

'Oh, sorry. Yes, Dad. But half eleven's not half the night, is it? Phil and his mates were off clubbing when I left them. They'd be out till after two.'

'I don't care what others do, Tim. Phillip Barraclough is eighteen and unemployed. He's not studying for G.C.S.E. I don't know why you want to hang around with lads that age, anyway.'

'We don't hang around, Dad. We go in MacDonald's or the Acropolis and talk, that's all. Drink coffee. And I go because Chris goes, and Phil's his brother.'

His mother dumped a spoonful of marmalade on her plate and looked at him. 'Yes, and that's another thing, Tim. Christopher Barraclough. We wish you wouldn't spend so much of your time with him.'

'What's wrong with him, Mum? Chris is my best friend.'

'He's a bad influence, Tim. He drinks and he's not all that keen on school. I've seen him in town in the middle of the afternoon, looking half doped. I hope he's not taking you with him, that's all.'

'Have you seen me?'

'No, but I'm not there all the time, am I? Your dad and I just wish you were more like your sister, Tim. She concentrated on her school work and look at her now – in Edinburgh, studying medicine.'

Tim clenched his fists under the table. Here we go. I knew we'd get round to this. Rebecca this, your sister that, Becky the other. I get it at school, I get it at home, it makes me want to puke.

'Can I leave the table, please?' He got up without waiting for permission and strode out of the kitchen.

## MYSTERIOUS MISTER

He went to the attic. The old refuge. The place he'd always been able to retreat to when grownups became unbearable. They'd both done it, Becky and himself, when they were small. Before she got all swotty and snotty and shut him out of her life, years before she went away.

She'd started it. The attic game. The secret, never-ending game they'd played together since before Tim could remember. Older by four years, she must have started bringing him up here before he could manage the stairs. Carrying him. Plonking him down on the floor. Telling him, long before he was capable of understanding, that this was Alpenland, their very own kingdom.

Rebecca was queen, of course, and no doubt in the beginning he'd been whatever she wanted him to be, but his earliest recollection was of refusing to be a dwarf. He was four at the time and his sister hadn't realised he'd know what a dwarf was. After all, she'd persuaded him to play a pig before, and a worm and a monster and a halfwit and a pile of dung. But now he was four and going to playschool and there was a book at playschool with a dwarf in it.

The parts he was offered after that tended to improve in direct proportion to his size and strength, until, in honour of his ninth birthday, Rebecca made him her consort, and joint ruler of Alpenland.

It was to be a brief reign. One day, only a few weeks later, out of the blue and for no reason he could fathom, she'd turned on him screeching when he suggested an ascent into Alpenland. Alpenland was stupid. It didn't exist. She'd got the name off a cereal packet and she was never going near that dirty attic again, so there.

She never did. Alpenland wasn't the same without her – especially now that he knew where the name came from – and so he let it go. After that the attic became a dungeon, a cavern, a Wellington bomber, and finally what it was now – a place of refuge from others, and from himself.

He mooched about, picking things up and putting them down. Relics of his parents' life. Of his and Rebecca's lives, too, when they were small. He wished it was like that now. He'd almost worshipped her, and now they'd turned his love into hate.

He squatted, shifting a pile of old clothes. There was a photograph underneath, in a frame. It was brown. A long-ago wedding picture. A bride in a long white dress, her hand hooked through the arm of a stiff-looking man with a dark suit and polished shoes. The frame had been silver once but it was brown now, like the photograph. The whole thing was loose, too – the dusty glass slipped about in the frame, and the back was coming away, and when Tim put it back on the floor it fell apart.

He straightened up and was moving away when he noticed that a bit of card, which somebody must have slipped in between the photograph and the backing, had a picture on it. He bent down and picked it up.

The card was thick. Age had cracked and browned its edges. On one side were some stains which might have been caused by water, and some badly faded pencil

7

marks. On the other side, in profile, somebody had drawn the head and shoulders of a man.

Tim ran a finger across the picture. It was an actual drawing, not a print. He could feel the indian ink standing up off the surface of the card.

He took it over to the grimy skylight and tilted it so that the light fell on it. The pencil marks looked like initials – AP or AR – and a year: 1935. A stain had all but obliterated the first two figures so that it might have been 1835, but Tim didn't think this likely. He turned the card over and examined the portrait. It gave him a funny feeling because it seemed oddly familiar. Maybe he'd seen it before, when he was a kid. Maybe Becky took the frame apart, then put it back. Or perhaps the man was like somebody he knew. Funny feeling anyway. Creepy.

He put the card in his jeans pocket and went downstairs.

# O Glorious Glass

Tabby found me, lying senseless on the half landing. She forced her dear, oft-bitten fingers between my teeth to prevent my biting my tongue, and called for assistance. My father came, and together they half-dragged, half-carried me to my bed; whereupon I recovered as usual, being left with the usual headache.

Some hours have passed, I think. My father was with me for a while, caressing my forehead, murmuring, 'My poor boy, my poor, poor boy,' over and over again, as he is wont to do on these occasions. It is now quite dark outside, and I am alone. The family will be gathering in the dining room for the evening meal.

I cannot face them. Not now. Nobody would mention my filthy affliction, of course – it is unmentionable – but it will be in their thoughts and those thoughts would show through the eyes they'd turn on me. Mad. Our brother, nephew, son. Mad.

Well, I'll show them. All of them. I've spoken with Robinson and the thing's practically settled. They'll be proud of me yet.

I lay on my back in the dark with my eyes closed and my hands behind my head and thought about the city in the glass. I became convinced that I had been granted a prophetic vision – a vision of London where, if all went according to plan, I should soon be going. Fame, I was now certain, awaited me there.

I roused myself, rose from my bed and lit a candle. I took pen and paper and began to write. I wrote, read what I had written, crossed it through and sat for a time, gazing into the flame before trying again. I repeated the process four times and still I wasn't satisfied. I can do better, I told myself. Far better. I know that I have it in me to become a great poet – one of the greatest. I tilted the paper to catch the light, and read.

> O glorious glass, that givest to me
> The sights that make my heaven,
> Such forms as theirs could never be
> By real mirror given.

Well – I was tired. Tomorrow, refreshed, I'd concentrate better. I'd finish the poem, and tell my father of my plan to go to London. That fame awaited me I now had no doubt. The only question was whether it would find me first through my poetry, or my painting.

Both, I told myself. Probably. I remember I blew out the candle and smiled in the dark. Then we shall see who's mad, shan't we?

# NEXT TIME I PASS

Tim stood in the kitchen doorway. His mother was scrubbing potatoes at the sink. The outside door was open, which probably meant his dad was in the drive-way, tinkering with the car in the spring sunshine.

'Hey, Mum?'

His mother looked round. 'Oh, so you've got over the sulks, have you?'

Tim shook his head. 'I wasn't sulking.'

'You could have fooled me.'

'I get fed up of being compared with Becky all the time, that's all. I'm me, Mum. I don't know how to be anybody else.'

'Oh, Tim.' She mopped her hands with a tea towel and gave him a quick hug. 'We don't want you to be anybody else. We love you. It's because we love you that your dad and I are concerned about you. We like to know how you're getting on at school. Who your friends are. Where you go in the evenings. We don't want to run your life, but we think we ought to pop in now and then to see how you're running it yourself.' She smiled. 'Okay?'

He grinned wryly and shrugged. 'I suppose so, Mum. I'm sorry I walked out like that. Look,' He drew the rectangle of card from his pocket. 'I found this in the attic. D'you know who it is, by any chance?'

His mother finished wiping her hands before taking the card. She frowned at the picture for a moment, then shook her head.

'No idea, love, I'm sorry. Where was it?'

'In the back of an old photo frame. It fell apart and this dropped out.'

'What was the photo?'

'Wedding. Ancient, by the look of it. You know – one of those brown ones.'

'Yes. I think it must be one of your grandma's old photos, Tim – part of the stuff we brought here when Grandad died and she moved to the flats. She probably put this in to pack out the frame or something, but I doubt she'd remember now. It must have been a long time ago, and anyway your grandad might have done it.'

'It says 1935 on the back. Or 1835.'

His mother examined the pencil marks. 'Hmm. Difficult to say. Not 1835 though, surely?' She looked at the portait again, holding it at arm's length, then at Tim. She smiled. 'Oddly enough he's not unlike you, Tim. Similar sort of profile. Even the specs are like yours.'

'Oh, thanks a lot, Mum!' He plucked the card from her fingers and studied it. 'My nose isn't that size for a start.' He looked at her. 'Is it?'

His mother laughed. 'Well, yes, love, I'm afraid it is. You've probably never seen yourself in profile. We don't, usually.' She noticed his expression and said, 'Hey – there's no need to look so down in the mouth, Tim. There's nothing wrong with your looks, for goodness sake.'

11

'Isn't there?' He stuffed the card back in his pocket. 'You wouldn't exactly call me the most handsome guy in the western hemisphere though, would you? I mean even you wouldn't, and you're my mother.'

'Well, that's the whole point, Tim. I'm your mother, and look at me.' She flicked up two handfuls of her hair and let them fall. 'Frizzy ginger hair. Freckles. Piggy little eyes that can't see straight and a nose like the front end of a canoe. D'you think I didn't hate the way I looked when I was young? I used to sit at my dressing table and cry, but there was nothing I could do about it. We get our looks from our parents, and at least you inherited some of your dad's as well as some of mine.'

'Big deal. You talk as if Dad was Sylvester Stallone or somebody. You don't think he might know who this is, do you?'

She shook her head. 'No. I told you, your grandma might know. It's a long shot, but you could always pop over there and ask her. She'd be pleased to see you.'

'I know.' His mother was always trying to get him to visit his grandma, but the block of sheltered flats she lived in was right across town, and anyway the old lady tended to talk about Becky all the time, too. 'I'm not making a special trip, Mum. I might bob in and ask her the next time I pass.'

'But you never pass, Tim.'

'Then I'll never know, Mum, will I?'

# DOWN WITH A BANG

As soon as lunch was over, Tim slipped out to phone Dilys. The Souths had their own phone, but Dilys was a sort of secret, and so was some of the stuff he might decide to tell her about last night.

Last night. He grinned, sauntering down to the corner in the warm sunshine. It hadn't been MacDonalds, like he told his dad. It hadn't been the Acropolis, either. They'd gone to Grobs, him and Chris and Phil and a few others. Grobs was a wine bar. You weren't supposed to go in under eighteen but nobody bothered. Chris and himself were probably the youngest boys there, but some of the girls were younger. Thirteen. Well, no more than fourteen, anyway.

They'd had a great time, sitting in the semi-darkness round some tables they pulled together, sipping wine, smoking, listening to music and chatting up the girls. He wouldn't be saying anything to Dilys about the girls, of course. Guys like him – guys who really know what's what – play it cool. Which means they can have a good time without blabbing about it all over town, right? Cool and easy does it every time.

He'd done all right. Better than all right, in fact. He'd been suave. Dead suave. And they were all over him, weren't they – lapping it up? He'd had to leave at half ten to give the others a chance.

He stood in the callbox and punched out the Williams's number.

'Scorton 42972.'

'Oh, hello, Mrs Williams. Tim here. Can I speak to Dilys, please?'

'Who?'

'Dilys.'

'No, I mean who are you?'

'Oh, sorry. Tim. Tim South. Dilys and I are in the same class.'

'D'you think so? Hold on a minute.'

Cowbag. She had her hand over the mouthpiece but he could hear her calling her daughter. There was a scraping noise and some whispering, then Dilys came on. 'Hello?'

'Oh, hi – she finally let you have it, then?'

'Who? What you on about?'

'Your mother. I heard her. Who is it. What does he want. Tell her it's the phantom flasher of Linley Park, ringing for a date.'

'Don't talk so daft, Tim South. And where were you last night anyway – we waited hours.'

'That's what I'm phoning about. I met Chris and Phil and some other lads and we went to Grobs.'

'Charming. So Cheryl and Gary and me could have sat waiting all night in MacDonald's for all you cared. Is that it?'

'You know it's not, Dil. That's why I phoned.'

'Yes, well you needn't have bothered because I don't want to talk to you. And don't call me Dil. Don't call me at all, in fact.'

The receiver went down with a bang. Tim stood for a moment, gazing at the dead instrument in his fist, then hung up and left the box.

That wasn't how it was supposed to go at all, he told himself. She was supposed to be glad I called. I thought I'd apologise in this really dignified voice, and then she'd say oh, that's all right Tim – I know I can't expect you to spend all your free time with me, and I'm glad you called. Where did you get to, anyway? Grobs – oh wow! I bet you had a great time. And then I'd have told her all about it— .

Would I? He kicked a pebble, viciously, so that it went skittering across the road. All about it? All? What about the ginger dwarf bit – would I have told her that? How the girls latched on to the other guys and ignored me so that I was thinking of leaving, and then one of them looked at me and giggled and said, 'Who's the ginger dwarf?' And I said I had to go to the gents and went out the back way, crying? Would I have told Dilys that? Dilys, the only girl who doesn't mind being seen with me in public. Didn't, I should say, because I've lost her now, haven't I? How's this for a lyric, then:

> *Hey girls, run and see –*
> *Suave, the ginger dwarf, that's me.*

Good, eh?


# ONE OF THE GANG

'Hey, Chris – wait on.'

Monday, three forty-five. Hometime. Chris turned. Tim put a spurt on and caught him halfway down the drive.

'What d'you reckon to this trip, then?'

Their English group was doing *Jane Eyre* for G.C.S.E. and old Ellis had sprung a trip on them. He was planning to take them to Haworth for a week at the end of May. You don't have to go, he'd told them, but we'll be staying at a youth hostel and it won't all be poking about in museums. You'll all have been revising furiously, and it'll be a break for you before the exams; you know – like football managers sometimes take their teams to the Bahamas or somewhere in the middle of a tough cup campaign so they can wind down a bit. They get a break from training, come back relaxed and get to Wembley.

Chris grinned. 'I'm going. It's a week out of school, isn't it? How about you?'

Tim shrugged. 'Dunno. I mean, I can't see how walking round the place where a book was written is going to help you answer questions about it.'

'It isn't, you div, but who cares? It's a week away from this dump, and when we get back we'll only have six weeks to do. Think of it, Timmo – no more school!'

'It's all right for you, Chris. Your folks know you're leaving. Mine are expecting me to stay on. A-levels. University. All that. School till I'm about twenty-five, then a brilliant career.' He pulled a face. 'I've got to match up to my sister, haven't I?'

'And what about you?' Chris demanded. 'It's your life, isn't it? What do you want to do?'

'Me?' Tim shook his head. 'I don't know, Chris. I can't decide. I want to leave, really, I suppose – be one of the gang with you and Phil and the others – but my parents'll go mad if I do. Anyway, I've got to make my mind up because I've an interview with Dusty tomorrow and I know he'll be twisting my arm to stay on.'

'Tell him to naff off,' said Chris.

Tim smiled wryly. 'Like I said, Chris – it's all right for you.'

# A Talent Like Yours

At breaktime on Tuesday morning, Tim parked his body outside Dusty Miller's door and left it there while he went to be interviewed by Sir Robert Maxwell.

\*

He knocked. Sir Robert told him to come in. He did. 'Ah,' smiled the great man. 'Mr. South, isn't it?'

'Yes, Sir,' said Tim.

'Mr Tim South?'

'Yes, sir.'

Sir Robert nodded towards a chair in front of his gigantic desk. 'Grab a pew then, Tim. Cigar?'

'I don't smoke, sir.'

'Good man! Now then, when was it you joined us here at the *Mirror*, Tim?'

'Last week, sir.'

'Last week. And in what capacity are you employed?'

'Office boy, sir.'

'Office boy.' Sir Robert chuckled and pushed a tattered notebook towards him. 'This is yours, I believe?'

Tim looked at the notebook. 'It looks like mine, sir, but—?'

'How do I come to have it?' Sir Robert chuckled again. 'You left it lying around, lad. Somebody picked it up – never mind who – and flicked through it, looking for the owner's name. Well, she found it. And she found something else as well. D'you know what else she found, Tim?'

17

'No, sir.' His heart lurched. Had something terrible slipped in between the pages of his notebook? Was he about to get the sack? He looked anxiously at his employer. Sir Robert returned his gaze, and there was a twinkle in his eye. 'She found six of the punchiest, most penetrating pieces of journalism she'd ever seen, Tim. How did you come to write these?'

'Oh,' said Tim, faintly. 'I – just sort of scribble, sir – in my lunch hours and coffee breaks. It's a sort of hobby, sir.'

'A sort of hobby.' Sir Robert tapped the notebook with a beautifully manicured nail. 'Well, I'll tell you, Tim – a talent like yours occurs about once every century – if that often – and when it does, it deserves better than to be hidden away in some poky little office. How'd you like to edit one of my papers?'

Tim goggled. 'Me, sir – an editor? Are there any sixteen-year-old editors, sir?'

Sir Robert laughed. 'There are now. One, anyway. How does eighty thousand a year grab you?'

'It grabs me, sir. When do I start?'

'What time is it now?'

'Ten past nine, sir.'

'Start at ten, then – no use rushing things. Oh, and one more thing, Tim.'

'Yessir?'

His employer gave him a warm smile. 'Call me Bob, okay?'

*

'Come on in, Tim.' He got back into his body and propelled it into Dusty's room. 'Sit down.' He sank onto the small, hard chair in front of Dusty's cluttered desk. 'Now then.' The teacher rubbed his dry old hands together briskly. 'I hope you've been thinking seriously

18

about your future since our last talk, Tim?'

What, no cigar? 'Yes, sir.'

'Good. And what do you think you'd like to do?'

'I'm leaving, sir.'

'What?'

'I'm leaving, sir. At the end of this term. I'll be sixteen then.'

'Oh, Tim!' The teacher looked distressed. 'I know you'll be sixteen, but what about qualifications? A levels? You won't get to university on G.C.S.E.s, you know.'

'I don't want to go to university, sir.'

'You don't want—.' Dusty looked at him as though he's said he no longer wanted his head. 'But your sister, Tim – Rebecca – she's at university, isn't she? I mean, have you discussed this with your parents?'

'No, sir. There's no point. I know what they'd say, but it's my life, not theirs.'

'I thought you fancied journalism, Tim. You wrote off to some editors, didn't you?'

'Yessir.'

'And?'

Tim sighed. 'It was no good, sir. You've either got to go to university, or start as a junior reporter on some local rag, doing funerals and flower shows and stuff.'

'Well, of course you have, Tim. Everybody's got to start somewhere. What did you expect, for heaven's sake?'

Tim shrugged. 'I dunno. Not funerals and flower shows, that's for sure. I wanted to report crime, sir, or football, or – you know – wars and that. World affairs.'

Mr Miller sighed, shaking his head. 'Experience, Tim. Experience. Journalism's a trade, and like all trades it's got to be learned. Those special correspondents with their by-lines – they didn't start by reporting great events. Some went to university. Others did funerals and flower shows. Nobody starts at the top, Tim.'

'But I could, sir. I know I could. I read their stuff all the time, and it's no better than I can do. I need a chance to prove it, sir – that's all.'

The teacher gazed at him. 'D'you suppose, Tim, that Sir Robert Maxwell sits in his office all day, hoping that someone like you – a sixteen-year-old straight out of school – will come knocking on his door so that he can appoint him editor of the *Daily Mirror* or something?'

Tim nodded. 'Yes, sir.'

'What? Are you being insolent, South?'

'No, sir. That's exactly what I suppose, sir. I was supposing it outside your door just now. You must be psychic, sir.'

'And you, South, must be living in cloud cuckoo land. I shall write to your parents. You can go now.'

*

Tim did nothing for the rest of the day. He couldn't concentrate. He kept trying to catch Dilys's eye, but she wouldn't look at him. He played back his session with Dusty, over and over again, unable to believe he'd said what he'd said. His dad was going to go mad when he got Dusty's letter. Leaving school and cheeking a teacher.

He kept thinking about something else as well, and he didn't know why. It was the picture. The one he'd found in the attic. The funny-looking guy with the big nose that Mum said looked like him. He'd put it out of sight in the drawer of his bedside unit, but he kept thinking about it.

# ILLICIT AMOURS

After tea, Tim excused himself and went to his room. He sat hunched on the bed with his elbows on his knees and his fists on his cheeks, staring at the carpet between his feet.

He was thinking about Dusty's letter. The old wassock was probably writing it at this very minute, in his crummy house overlooking Linley Park: exaggerating the incident, making it sound worse that it really was. Enjoying it. Later on – say around half six – he'd have it with him when he went off to Morris dancing or the varicose vein society or whatever boring thing he did at night. He'd post it, and it'd have a first class stamp on because he wouldn't be able to wait to get Tim in trouble.

Which means it'll arrive tomorrow morning. I could intercept it: pick up the mail and slip Dusty's letter in my pocket before Dad sees it. I know his writing.

No. He'd only write again, wouldn't he? Or phone. And then I'd be even deeper in trouble. Oh, heck!

He opened the drawer of his bedside unit, took out the picture and sat looking at it. Who were you, eh, with your whiskers and your high collar? I'm assuming you're dead now. Did you ever get yourself in a spot like this? Mind you – Tim smiled to himself – it doesn't matter if you did, does it? Not now, you lucky pig. I wouldn't half like to know who you were, though.

He stood up. No use worrying over Dusty's stupid letter. I'd have had to tell Dad sooner or later that I'm leaving anyway, and he'd have gone ape-shape, same as he will when he gets it. Just have to face it – get it over with. He slipped the picture in his pocket and left the room.

It was across town, where his gran lived. An old folks' flat in a block with a lot of others. Celandine House, it was called. Just inside the door was a little cubicle with someone on duty. You had to tell her who you were visiting, and she'd buzz them and ask if they wanted to see you. They could buzz her too, if they needed help or anything. It was like Alcatraz or somewhere, and there was always a funny smell in the corridors.

Gran's pad was one floor up. Tim took the lift. There were spy-holes in everybody's door. The old lady looked through hers, then let him in.

She was pleased to see him. It had been a long time. How was his mother, and that clever sister of his. How was he getting on at school. Of course, school wasn't like that when she was young. You were frightened of your teachers in those days. They didn't hesitate to use the cane, and it never did anybody any harm. Kids today didn't know they were born, and what did they do. Went round terrorising old folks and smashing things up, that's what. Touch of the cane's what they wanted. That'd stop 'em. Or the cat. Couple of years in the army. Would he like a cup of tea.

They sipped tea. Tim took the picture out of his pocket and handed it to his grandmother. 'D'you know who this is, Gran?'

The old lady looked at it, then at him. 'Yes, Tim. As a matter of fact I do, but where on earth did you find this? I haven't seen it for years – since before you were born, I shouldn't wonder.'

Tim told her about the photograph in the attic. His gran nodded. 'My parents, Tim, on their wedding day. 1914. Your great grandparents. My dad, Willy, was

22

killed in the Great War, and my mother died before you were born. Her name was Constance and she had T.B. – consumption, they called it then. I wondered what had happened to that photo.'

'And what about that, Gran?' He nodded towards the card.

'Well – I suppose I must have put this behind the photo at some time to tighten it up, but I don't remember. I know what it is, though. My mother told me, but I'm not sure I ought to tell you, Tim.'

'Why not?'

The old lady chuckled. 'Because it involves a scandal, young man – the skeleton in our family cupboard.'

Tim grinned. 'I'm fifteen, Gran. I know all about illicit amours, if that's what it is.'

'Do you indeed? When I was fifteen, I still thought they found babies under gooseberry bushes. Anyway, you're right about the illicit amour, as you call it, because this is the man who ruined my great, great grandmother.'

'Your — '. Tim looked at her. 'How the heck would you know that, Gran? Your great, great grandmother? It must have been centuries ago.'

'One and a half centuries, Tim, that's all. 1835.'

'Hey!' Tim grinned. 'You're spot on, Gran. It says 1835 on the back, only I thought it was 1935.'

He frowned. 'How do you know about it – is it written down or something?'

The old lady shook her head. 'Certainly not, Tim. I told you – it's the family scandal. Who'd put a thing like that on paper? No – my mother told me the story when she showed me this portrait, just as her mother had told her. They've been handed down, you see – the picture and the story, from one generation to the next, ever since 1835.'

Tim shook his head. 'It's hard to believe, just the same. You didn't pass it on to Mum, because she doesn't know anything about the picture – I asked her.'

'No, well – it was all a very long time ago, Tim. I thought it best to let it drop, but here it is, so perhaps we're meant to keep it going. D'you want to hear the story?'

'Sure. I want to know who he is, don't I?'

'He's your great, great, great, great grandfather, Tim. That's who he is, the wicked man.'

'Yes, I know, but who was he? What was his name. It says AP or AR on the back.'

'Oh, I can't tell you that. Nobody knows. All I know is, he was an artist. A student at the Royal Academy in London. Clare Connor – the girl who became my great great grandmother – was Irish. She'd come to London looking for work. She worked in a pub. He came in and swept her off her feet. Gave her a false name, a baby and this likeness of himself, then vanished.' She chuckled. 'A rogue, Tim, that's what he was, but if it wasn't for him I'd not be here, and neither would you. Funny old world, isn't it?'

Tim plucked the portrait from her fingers and looked at it. 'An artist, eh? D'you think he was famous, Gran?'

The old lady shook her head. 'I doubt it, Tim. He was just a student.'

'He could have got famous later, though, couldn't he? I mean, we don't know his name or anything. Just think – I might be the great, great, great, great grandson of a famous artist. His pictures might be worth millions now. Hey!' He waved the bit of card. 'This one might!'

His grandmother smiled. 'Well, if you get a million

24

for it, Tim, I'll expect you to treat me to a holiday in the Bahamas.'

Tim grinned. 'It's a deal. I'll see you later, Gran – okay?'

He walked back across town, dreaming all the way.

## AT THE BULL

It's all arranged. Robinson's managed so many letters of introduction for me we'll be obliged to take the carrier's cart, for I swear they'll not fit in the gig.

I'm to go at the end of August. The whole house is abuzz with it and it's the talk of the village, too. Father has spoken with Robinson, who has agreed to accompany me. We'll be lodging at the Chapter Coffee House in Paternoster Row, where my father often stayed in his youth.

All these preparations have induced in me a state of such delighted anticipation, such hope, that I would not have believed it possible anything could increase my felicity; yet increased it is, by something John Brown told me this evening at the Bull.

It seems that that incomparable former practitioner of the pugilistic art, Tom Spring, now keeps a tavern at Holborn known as the Castle, and a most excellent establishment it is, according to an acquaintance of John's. Spring has long been a hero of ours, and John has insisted that while I am in London I must seek the fellow out and shake his hand. I can scarce contain my impatience to be off!

Not that my stay in the capital will be all pleasure by any means. Earlier today, Robinson was doing his best to batter down my soaring spirit with talk of going into anatomy, and something called study from the antique, which consists in making hundreds of drawings from some marbles at the British Museum. Apparently all this is part of the Royal Academy's entry requirement for would-be students, but I suspect they'll waive much of it when they see my work. And if they do not, why then I'll fulfil their dull requirement and be damned!

I wonder – how will London take to me?

## OUT OF YOUR SKULL

Tim didn't feel a bit like school next morning. For one thing it was Wednesday – a long way from last weekend, a long way to next. Also, it was the day his dad would be getting Dusty's letter. The mail hadn't arrived when Tim set off, and his father had left before him, which meant it would all happen at teatime. Something to spend the long day looking forward to.

Then there was Dilys. He'd been keen on her for ages, but it's not easy to ask a nice looking girl out when you're a ginger dwarf and a daft little four-eyed gitt as well, and it had taken him about six months to get himself together and approach her. When he finally did, it turned out she quite liked him, which was amazing. Since then they'd spent a lot of time together, walking to and from school and meeting sometimes in the evenings and at weekends. Their parents didn't know, but there was no reason why they should – they weren't about to run off and get married or anything. They liked each other, that's all.

And he'd blown it. Blown it for the sake of a packet of fags and a couple of drinks in Grobs. Cheryl and Gary, Dilys and himself. They'd have grabbed a table at MacDonalds and talked over cokes and maybe shared a bag of chips. After, they'd have split up for the walk home. Nothing mind-blowing. Just two couples having a quiet night out.

Now, as he came to the place where he and Dilys usually met for the walk to school, he hung about with his hands in his pockets, looking along her road. It was twenty to nine. They usually met around quarter to, so she should be along any minute. He didn't know what he'd say to her, or if she'd let him say anything at all, but he couldn't go on not seeing her. He had to give it a try.

She appeared just before quarter to, walking alone. She must have seen him and she could have gone round the other way, but she didn't. She came on with her head down, not looking at him.

When she seemed about to pass by he said, 'Hi.'

She gave him a sideways glance and said, 'Hi,' then walked on without slackening her pace.

Tim trotted after her. 'Hey, Dil – hang on a minute – I want to talk.'

'You could've talked all night, Saturday.'

'I said I was sorry, Dil. Yesterday. On the phone.'

'Yes, and I said don't call me Dil, didn't I!'

'Aw, come on – give me a chance, hey?'

'Get lost, Tim.'

'We can talk, can't we? As we go along? That won't kill you, will it?'

'All right then – talk.' She kept on, head down, hands in pockets, face like thunder. He hurried along beside her.

'Listen, Dil. I'm in trouble, right? I had this interview with Dusty. Careers interview. I told him I was leaving.'

'You're crazy, Tim South. You're not leaving. Your folks wouldn't let you.'

'Yes I am, Dil. They don't run my life.'

'Well, who does then, Tim? Not you, that's for sure. You don't know what you want. It's only about three weeks since you were giving me a lot of stuff about being a journalist. You were even writing off to editors, for Pete's sake – what happened?'

'They want graduates, Dil.'

'So what's wrong with going to university? I thought that was the idea.'

Tim shook his head. 'Not now. I'm fed up with school. I want to get out there and do something.'

'Like what?' She was brusque but her pace had slackened. She was listening.

'Like being a special correspondent or a TV reporter or maybe an editor.'

Dilys looked at him. 'Did you say this to Dusty?'

'Yes.'

'And what did he say?'

Tim shrugged. 'Nothing much. Went on about experience. I told him I didn't need it.'

'You're out of your skull, Tim. D'you know that? No wonder you're in trouble.'

'I don't care, Dil. It's true – I can write as well as any of them, but I got carried away and told Dusty he was psychic. He's written to my dad.'

They had reached the school gateway. It was nearly

five to nine. Kids were straggling up the drive. Bikes swerved in and out among them. Dilys stopped.

'Look, Tim. I'm sorry you're in trouble, but really you've brought it on yourself. I don't know why you wanted to tell me about it, but if you want to know what I think, it's this. I think you should stay on like me and get your A levels and go to university and be a journalist. You'd be a good one – you're brilliant at English. Go tell Dusty you've changed your mind.' She looked at him. 'Okay?'

Tim pulled a face. 'I dunno, Dil. I'd probably never make it, anyway. I'm awkward around people. How can you be a journalist if you're awkward around people?

Dilys snorted, tossing her head. 'One minute you're bragging, and the next you're saying you'll never make it. You want to make your mind up, Tim South!' She spun on her heel and flounced off up the drive.

Tim stood for a moment gazing after her, then followed. That's no great trick, he told himself. Making your mind up. The hard bit's how to be the guy you wish you were.

# TIMMY THE KID

The first thing Tim saw when he got back from school that afternoon was Dusty's letter on the hall table. Buff envelope, first class stamp, A. South, Esq in Dusty's Dead Sea scrawl. His Mum had picked it off the mat without knowing what it was and left it because it was addressed to her husband. Tim pulled a face at it and went through to the kitchen.

'Lo, Mum.' His mother was washing lettuce at the sink. She worked mornings as secretary at the local infant school and did her wife and mother bit in the afternoons. She looked round.

'Hello, Tim. Good day?'

Tim shrugged. 'All right.'

'You sound a bit down, love. What's wrong?'

'Nothing. I don't feel too good, that's all. I think I'll skip tea and go sit in the attic if that's all right.'

'I suppose you had burgers and chips and coke for lunch again, didn't you? Sugar, grease and chemicals. Then you wonder why you're off your food. Ugh!'

'I had a ham salad, Mum. And a glass of milk and an orange. I'll be okay if I just sit quiet for a bit.' Maybe Dad'll go a bit easy, he thought, if he knows I'm feeling rough.

In the attic he sat on a suitcase full of bedding and gazed at Silver, the rocking-horse. He'd loved that thing once. Stroked it. Whispered his secrets in its ear and believed himself heard. He tried to recapture some shred of the old affection and found that he couldn't even imagine it. Growing up sucks, he thought.

\*

It was probably the horse that did it, but whatever it was he found himself walking slow and easy across a typical western saloon in dusty Levis with the forty-five banging his thigh every second stride. Rough men and scantily dressed women watched from little tables. Somebody whispered 'Timmy the Kid', and a thin man in shirtsleeves got up from the piano stool and scuttled into the backroom.

The bartender was nervous, too. 'H-h-hi, Kid,' he stammered, 'What'll you have?'

'Gimme an orange,' growled Tim, 'and a glassa milk.'

'Sure, Kid,' said the bartender, and then, somewhere in the silent room, somebody laughed.

Tim grew very still. He stood with both hands resting lightly on the bar, looking in the fancy mirror. He stayed like that so long, everybody thought he'd missed the laugh. They started to relax. Then, slowly, the Kid turned. His hands hung loose at his sides. His eyes swept the room and came to rest on a thickset man who looked like the actor Ed Begley, and who badly needed a shave and a change of clothes. He was sitting between two girls in their underwear, but as Tim's eyes picked him out the girls got up and backed off, watching the gunman through wide, mascara-ed eyes. Tim fixed his victim with a baleful stare.

'Something funny, fella?'

The man's face paled and twitched. Spangles of sweat stood out on his forehead. He was as good as dead and he knew it. He clutched the arms of his chair and pushed it back with a harsh scraping sound. His eyes never left the Kid's. As soon as he had the space he lurched to his feet and went for his gun.

He never had a chance. His hand had scarcely brushed the butt when the Kid drew and fired. The bullet struck him in the chest and he performed a backward somersault over the chair, which fell to pieces. The Kid gazed at the corpse for a moment, holstered the smoking Colt and reached for his milk. Nobody laughed.

*

'Timothy!' At the sound of his father's voice the saloon vanished and Tim found himself sitting unarmed on a suitcase full of old bedding. He groaned and clambered to his feet.

'Coming, Dad.' Oh boy, he thought. Here we go. He

31

glanced across at the rocking horse. 'Where are you, old pal,' he murmured, 'now that I need you?'

# KEEPING IT HID

God, how this place stinks in summer! Today has been the sixth of May, and the sun has shone all day, drawing forth noisome vapours from cottage dungheaps and from the cloaca beneath the main street. How I long to shake the village dust from my feet and begone.

The sixth of May! Three months more to fester. Three and a half to be precise. Euphoria is overthrown. Impatience reigns.

The Bull has the cure for what ails me. I am assured by those who ought to know that a man in his cups does not notice the passage of time. The trouble is I daren't be seen near the place, for I'm a member of the local Temperance Society. As a child of the Manse my membership is all but obligatory as an example to others, or so my father says. And since toping and keeping it hid is not possible here, I have been forced to seek another way to skin the proverbial cat. In short, I have recently taken to calling upon the village apothecary, who sells me an elixir which, though it affects both mind and body in a most extraordinary way, is by no means forbidden to members of the Temperance Movement.

I refer of course to opium, source of De Quincy's inspiration and driver, for me, of time's winged chariot. I consider it prudent to keep the thing secret from those about me, and, since the stuff comes in small bottles it is a simple matter to smuggle it up to my room. You would not believe the alteration those little bottles have wrought in my life! I sit, or lie, for hours at a time in a state of imperturbable bliss, while visions of the most fantastical sort come and go about me. Ideas for poems – unutterably beautiful poems in which I expound life's most profound truths, swirl in my head, and I am able to conjure my city – my city in the glass – my Verdopolis – at will. I have found another world, and I plan to dwell there till the time which lies between my dream and its fulfilment has passed.

# GAP IN THE WALL

In the twelve seconds it took Tim to get down the attic stairs he played out this fantasy:

\*

His father is on the landing, looking up the stairs. He has Dusty's letter in his hand and an angry expression on his face. Tim descends briskly. You sense his strength, his determination. He confronts his father and before the older man can utter a word, jabs a finger at him and says, 'Listen – I know what you're going to say and you're wasting your time. It's my life, I'll do what I damn like with it, and you'll stay the hell outa my way if you know what's good for you.'

\*

His father was on the landing, looking up the stairs. He did have Dusty's letter in his hand and an angry expression on his face. Tim did come down, but his rate of descent was not brisk, and a spectator would have needed a pretty vivid imagination to sense either strength or determination in his manner. He blinked innocently at the older man. 'You wanted to see me, Dad?'

His father looked dubious. 'Wanted to see you, Tim? Wanted to? I don't think I'd put it quite like that, no. Let's say that as your father I consider it my duty to speak to you about this.' He waved Dusty's letter in his son's face. 'I want to know why you were insolent to your teacher, and why you told him you were leaving school when you're not.'

'I wasn't insolent, Dad. He asked me a question and I answered it truthfully. It wasn't the answer he'd expected, that's all. And I am thinking of leaving.'

'Then you can jolly well think again, lad.'

'Why, Dad? I'm sick of school. It's boring, and anyway it's my life, isn't it?'

'Your life?' His father's lip curled. 'Oh, yes, it's your life all right. Never mind the years your mother and I have given out of *our* lives, bringing you up. Worrying about you. Working to give you a flying start. D'you suppose we've watched over you all these years so that you could end up hanging about on street corners, spitting?'

'I won't be hanging about on street corners spitting, Dad. I want to do something. Something in the real world, not school or university. I want to be somebody.'

'And do you really imagine that's the way to become somebody, Tim? To leave school at sixteen with a couple of G.C.S.E.s and join the dole queue? You're kidding yourself, my lad. It's a hard world out there – a jungle. You need qualifications if you're going to get anywhere. You're not leaving school, Timothy, till you've got two or three A levels under your belt and a place at a college or university. And as for this' – he waved the letter again – 'tomorrow morning you'll go to Mr Miller and you'll apologise for your insolence. Is that clear?'

Tim nodded. It was clear all right, but it wasn't going to happen. No way. He was damned if he was going to apologise for telling the truth, and he'd leave school if he wanted to as well. How to work it, that was the problem.

As soon as he could, Tim got his jacket from the hallway and slipped out of the house. He needed to cool off and think, and you can't beat a long walk by yourself for that. He turned left out of the gateway and strode along Anemone Way with his shoulders hunched and his hands in his pockets. At the end he turned left again, making his way down Broom Avenue towards the canal. It was a fine evening, dry and fairly warm, and there were a couple of hours of daylight left. Broom Avenue was a cul-de-sac, with a narrow gap in the wall at the bottom giving access to the towpath. The gap was just about wide enough to ride a motorbike through, and the council had planted a bollard in the middle to prevent this. Tim squeezed past the bollard and turned right.

He'd hoped to have the towpath more or less to himself but the weather had brought out dog walkers, elderly couples who'd probably done their courting here before the war, even families with pushchairs. Tim quickened his pace, and when he'd gone half a mile or so he'd left them all behind. There was still the odd angler hunched on the bank, but anglers have eyes only for the water and don't really count. As he slowed down, two damp joggers appeared ahead and passed him, heading back to town.

The towpath narrowed. Beyond the drystone wall to his right old sycamores grew thickly, their branches overhanging the canal. The dense foliage screened out most of the light, so that Tim seemed to be walking through a dim green tunnel. Some branches arched right over and dabbled their leaves in the water. Here and there, shafts of weak sunlight pierced the canopy and fell in pale dapples on the path. He was tramping along with his hands in his pockets, thinking rebellious thoughts, when he heard somebody call his name. He stopped. The sound seemed to come from the far bank. He looked across. There was no towpath on that side. Trees and rank undergrowth crowded right to the brink. And there beneath it lay the rotting hulk of a barge. Chris Barraclough was sitting on its blackened deck with his legs over the side and his feet in the water.

## Ten Feet Tall

Chris grinned, and beckoned with a jerk of his head. 'Come on, then. What're you waiting for – the Captain's launch?' There was giggling in the shadows.

Tim shrugged. He wasn't in the mood for company. Not even Chris's. 'Who've you got with you?'

'Who've I got?' The question seemed to strike Chris as funny because his voice cracked. He controlled it, just, but Tim could tell he was struggling. 'I've got our Phil, and Janis, and Alvin and Lee. I don't think I've got anybody else but I'll just check.' He turned, and Tim saw him begin to shake with laughter. 'Hey, folks,' he spluttered, 'That's right, isn't it – I haven't got anyone else?'

Tim heard noises – scraping and bumping and some laughter – then somebody whooped, 'Don't see anyone else, Chris.'

'Bit dark in here, though,' added a second voice.

'Yeah.' A girl this time. 'Can't be absolutely sure. Tell him we'll keep our eyes skinned.'

Tim frowned. 'What's going on, Chris – you all gone barmy or what?'

'Not us, mate. We're cool. It's everybody else that's barmy. Come on over and we'll show you the secret of happiness. You'll be ten feet tall.'

Tim hesitated. He didn't like cracks about his height and besides, there was something funny going on over there. Must be. Chris didn't usually talk like this. Perhaps they were drinking. Well, he told himself, one thing's for sure – whatever they're doing they're having more fun than I am. He gestured towards the dark water. 'How do I get across – walk?'

Chris laughed. 'That's after we show you the secret. There's a footbridge round the bend, remember? You want to get a move on and all, or we'll have used up all the happiness.' As he spoke there was a movement behind him and a hand appeared over his shoulder, holding a cigarette. Chris took the cigarette and put it between his lips. The hand withdrew. He closed his eyes and drew deeply on the cigarette so that the tip brightened. Tim stood for a moment, gazing across, then set off up the towpath.

Behind him, somebody laughed.

# Motley Crew

The hulk wasn't as close to the bank as it had looked from the other side. There was a four foot gap at the narrowest point, up near the bow. The barge wasn't lying on an even keel either, but listed quite sharply away from the bank, so that Tim had to do an upward leap to gain the deck. Then he had to jam his brakes on like a cartoon character on the brink of a precipice – to keep his feet from running him down the slope and over the side into the water. This performance caused great hilarity among the four who sat watching him from the rim of an open hatchway, astern. They clapped and cheered as he got his balance and began teetering gingerly along the canted deck towards them, his head and shoulders raked by overhanging foliage. As he approached he saw that they were passing the cigarette around.

When he reached them, Janis Clegg shuffled over to make room for him and he sat down between her and Lee Freeman with his legs down the hatch. Phil Barraclough leaned across and offered him the cigarette. He shook his head. 'No, thanks, Phil – I don't smoke.' Peering into the blackness between his feet he saw the glint of water. 'This thing's sinking, if you ask me.'

The elder Barraclough laughed. 'It's sunk already, you dummy – resting on the bottom. Been here years. What d'you mean, you don't smoke?'

'I just don't, Phil – it makes me feel pukey, y'know?'

'Ah yes, but you've never tried one like this, have you – a joint, I mean?'

'Is that a joint?' Tim squinted at the cigarette. It was

38

a thin, lumpy rollup. He knew what a joint was, of course, but this was the first time he'd seen one. No wonder they were all giggling and acting daft.

'Sure it's a joint. Here.' The older boy offered it again. Tim hesitated. Chris, sitting with his back to them and his legs over the side, twisted round. 'Go on, Tim – have a drag. That's where the happiness is, man.'

Happiness. Yes, well – he could certainly use a bit of that right now, what with Dusty Miller and Dad and all that. Janis, giggling, dug him with her elbow and whispered, 'Come on then, Prof – join the club.' They called him Prof sometimes because he was in the top stream for most things and they weren't. He knew they used the title mockingly but it pleased him. He took the cigarette and put the damp end between his lips. Phil nodded. 'That's it, matey – good, deep drag now.'

At first it made him nauseous. That'll be the tobacco, he told himself. Not used to it. He sat with his legs dangling and his head reeling, wondering if he'd remember to get his feet out of the way if he had to puke down the hole. The cigarette went round and round, and every time it was his turn he took it, though he felt wretched. Between drags he sat with his shoulders hunched, gripping the rim of the hatchway and gazing down into the black water. When the butt was so short it was scorching their lips, Phil rolled a fresh one. Chris finished dabbling his feet and joined them round the hatch. Tim breathed deeply, fighting nausea. The others chattered, giggled or stared blankly in front of them.

Presently Tim's nausea eased a little. He looked around at his companions and the phrase 'motley crew' occurred to him. He giggled. Pirates, he thought. That's what we are. Captain Barraclough and his motley crew. Barraclough, now. Do pirates have names like that?

Not in movies they don't. Not in books, either. Black Barraclough, scourge of the Spanish Main. He giggled again. The others were looking at him, digging one another in the ribs and winking. Well, let them.

Barraclough was a common enough name, wasn't it? There must have been at least one pirate called Barraclough. And Ramsbottom. What about that? Cecil Ramsbottom, buccaneer. Well, why not? People don't choose their career according to the sort of name they have, do they? So there must have been pirates called Nigel and estate agents called Bart. It stood to reason. He plucked at Phil's sleeve. 'Hey listen, Phil. Would you buy a house off—.' He clapped a hand over his mouth, spluttering.

The youth smiled indulgently. 'What you on about, kid? What house?'

'No, listen.' Tim controlled himself and said, 'Off an outfit called Black Bart Properties, P.L.C.?'

Phil grinned and ruffled the younger boy's hair. 'You're away aren't you, kiddo – stoned out of your skull?' Tim nodded and burst out laughing and then the others were laughing too – not at him, but with him. He could feel their approval, their acceptance of him. What was that Janis had said – join the club? Well, here he was – a member of the ten feet tall club, high and happy.

Phil rolled another joint and it went round. Somewhere beyond the trees the sun went down. Twilight settled on the still water, deepening. Laughter trickled away as each of the six withdrew to that secret place inside his head where nothing can follow.

Tim thought about tomorrow and Dusty Miller and both seemed too small, too far away to matter, and the ghost of a smile flickered about his mouth. He saw Becky as he always saw her now, reading alone at a table in a little room, and felt dreamily sad for a while. He thought about Dilys, and his grandmother in her flat, and the man in the picture he'd found – and then he was standing under trees in a churchyard somewhere, with rooks cawing and gravestones all round and a feeling of utter desolation in his breast.

It only lasted a moment but it was involuntary, and his disabled brain registered the difference so that afterwards he would remember, and know that he had conjured no such scene.

# WHERE WERE YOU?

Every high is followed by its low. That Thursday morning Tim was so low he could have walked under a skateboard without removing his hat. He hadn't slept much in spite of the dope. It had given him a really laid-back feeling on the boat and while he was strolling home with Chris and the others around half ten. He'd been dead cool in front of his parents, who would have had half a dozen fits apiece if they'd guessed his condition; but then when he got to bed and tried to sink way back into his mind he kept seeing that graveyard.

Now it was a quarter to nine and he was waiting for Dilys. Good old Dil. He didn't know why, but talking to her always made him feel better, even when she was mad at him. She showed up at around the usual time and sure enough, she *was* mad at him.

'Where were you last night?' she demanded, as soon

as she came in range. 'I phoned around eight and your mother said you were out. Didn't know where, or when you'd be back. You're getting hard to find, Tim South.'

He told her about the row with his dad and his towpath walk. He left out the middle bit and said he got back around ten-thirty.

Dilys was no fool. It was one of the things he liked about her. She eyed him narrowly. 'D'you expect me to believe you spent three hours just trogging along the towpath by yourself?'

'I was cooling down, Dil. Thinking.'

'I wish I could believe you, Tim. Come on – who did you meet and what did you do? You look like death warmed up.'

He told her, knowing what her reaction would be, and she didn't disappoint him.

'I've said it before,' she told him, 'and I'll say it again. You're crazy, Tim. I can't understand what you see in Janis and Alvin and the Barracloughs and all that lot. They're nothing but a bunch of plonkers. To go round with them's bad enough, but to let them turn you on to dope's just ridiculous.' She started walking faster. Her mouth was a thin line. Here we go again, he thought.

'Listen, Dil.' He was practically running. Fleetingly, he wondered whether perhaps it was Dilys rather than the lads who were making a fool of him. What would Phil think if he saw him trotting after her like something she had on a leash? Never mind that. Got to make her understand.

'Listen Dil, it's great, right? I wouldn't have believed it. One minute I was down – I mean really depressed – and the next I was ten feet tall – a winner.'

She stopped and faced him, fists on hips. 'Ten feet tall?' she grated. 'A winner? Are you blind, Tim South?

Haven't you seen the posters? The TV ads? Have you seen the kids in them – those sick, pathetic wrecks? Do they look ten feet tall to you? Do they look like winners? They're dying, Tim. Dying at sixteen and seventeen and eighteen. Is that what you want for yourself? Well, is it? You've got a good brain, Tim. Use it. Think, for goodness sake, instead of running after losers just because they call you Prof and laugh at your jokes.'

Direct hit. He followed her with his eyes as she hurried away. He was shaking. Direct hit, you cruel cow, only it's all right for you. You're pretty. People like you. You don't know what it's like to be runty and plain. No, not even plain. Ugly. You don't know what it's like. Everybody should get a turn at being popular but they don't. Everybody deserves to feel good sometimes – even ugly people, but it doesn't work like that. Not by itself. Some of us need help to feel good. To be ten feet tall for a while. You're pretty, Dil Williams, so you don't understand. You don't understand.

You do though. Oh, you do.


# I Told Him


He agonised till breaktime, then went and knocked on the staffroom door. Mrs Lightowler opened it and Tim asked for Mr Miller. She told him to wait and he did, thinking about last night on the boat. Twelve hours ago, stoned out of his mind, none of this had mattered nor ever would again, yet here he was. He saw now that it had been inevitable from the start – when you're fifteen and your dad orders you to do something you do it, one way or another. You've got to be high, on anger or on dope, to believe otherwise.

'Well?' When Dusty wanted to put somebody down he raised his shaggy eyebrows. They were practically in his hair as he gazed at Tim. Avoiding his eyes, Tim said, 'I – my dad got your letter, sir. He said to apologise about the other day. I'm sorry I said you were psychic, sir.'

'Yes. Well, that's all right then, South. And what about this business of your leaving us, eh?'

Leaving us. Makes it sound like school's my family and he's my uncle. That'll be the day. 'He says I've got to stay on, sir, so I suppose I will.'

'Well, that's hardly the spirit, South, is it? I mean, there'll be no point your staying on if you're going to feel resentful the whole time. Sixth form means a lot of hard work y'know, and more often than not you'll be expected to get on without supervision. It's a preparation for university, you see. Nobody forces university students to keep their noses to the grindstone. It's up to them. But then you'll know all about that because your sister's one, isn't she?'

'Yes, sir.' Oh boy – here we go.

'Speaking of Rebecca, how's she doing up at Edinburgh? Coping, I suppose?'

'Yes, sir.'

'Knew she would. Fine girl, your sister. Always was. You could do far worse than take a leaf out of her book, South, d'you know that?'

'Yes, sir, I know that.' It was rammed down my throat with my first solid food, you wassock. 'Can I go now, sir?'

'Yes, you can go. But I hope you're going to buckle

down and do some work, South. You've got a good brain, lad – all you have to do is use it.'

'You're getting to sound like Dil.'

'What? Did you say something, South?'

'I said, "Bet you a pound I will", sir.'

'Oh. Well. Splendid. Off you go, then.'

*

When half past three finally crawled round, Tim lingered in the cloakroom till most of the kids had gone. Dilys sometimes walked part of the way with him and for once he didn't want her company. Once he'd got his encounter with Dusty out of the way her words had played back over and over in his head, following him even when he tried to escape into fantasy.

When he got to the bottom of the drive, Phil and Alvin were there. Sometime last night he'd told them he was supposed to apologise to Dusty today, and that he wasn't going to. They'd obviously hung around to find out what happened, and he didn't feel like telling them because it wasn't much of a story. Still, never mind – most stories can be improved on with a bit of imagination, and imagination was one thing Tim had plenty of.

He grinned as they fell in beside him.

'Hi, lads.'

'Hi. How'd you go on with Dusty – did you apologise?'

'Did I heck! He came to the staffroom door, right? And I told him. I said my dad got your letter and I'm supposed to apologise but I'm not. I said for one thing, everything I said the other day was true, and for another it's my life and I decide whether I leave school or not.'

'You didn't!'

45

'I did. You should have seen his face. Talk about gob-smacked!'

Alvin chuckled with relish. 'And what did he say?'

Tim shrugged. 'What could he say? He just stood there for a bit with those eyebrows crawling up and down his head and his mouth open, then he muttered something about insolence and mentioning this to the Head and shut the door in my face.'

'Wow!' Admiration shone in Chris's eyes. 'That's beautiful, Timmo. I never thought you'd do it. What if he tells old Hurford, though?'

Tim shrugged again. 'I don't give a monkey's. If he sends for me I'll tell him the same thing I told Dusty – nobody runs my life but me.'

When their ways parted, both boys slapped him on the back and punched him in the arm and invited him to join them on the boat Saturday night. He told them he'd be there, and went on his way rejoicing.

There's more than one way of feeling ten feet tall.

# Dim Grim Rim

That night Tim had a dream. He was alone on the boat, dangling his legs down the hatch. It must have been late because the light was poor. He was looking into the hole, trying to see the water but it was too dark. He could hear it, though, sucking and gurgling down there in the blackness. He sat listening to it, and as he did so the sound shifted till it seemed to come from above. It

46

was different too – like somebody weeping. He looked up.

At the far side of the hatch, a small boy was standing. His shoulders were hunched, his hands covered part of his face and he rocked a little as he gazed, weeping softly, into the hole. As he stared at the child, Tim felt something damp and crumbly under his palms where the rim of the hatch had been. He looked down and saw that he was sitting on the edge of an open grave. In the grave lay a coffin so small it could only be a child's. Somewhere, rooks were calling, and the scent of fresh-turned earth was all around.

Awake, he lay damp and trembling. Darkness pressed down on his eyeballs and he smelled the earth. It was some time before he could bring himself to stir. When he did, it was to roll on his side and grope for the lamp on the bedside unit. When he had light he sat up, pulled open the drawer and took out the portrait. He tilted it towards the lamp and studied it, his lower lip caught between his teeth. Presently he shivered, returned the likeness to the drawer and lay down, pulling the covers right up to his chin. He left the light on, and it was a long time before he went to sleep.

# POPPY JUICE

One week more to bide, and I can scarcely believe it. Surely it was only yesterday that twelve weeks lay between my destiny and me? But no. There has been no mistake. Today's date is the ninth of September and the rest is poppy juice.

The day before yesterday my father wrote to Robinson to tell him that I shall go to him at Leeds on Friday to take my last lesson. I am to stay at his house overnight, and on Saturday morning the two of us will leave for London. The moment I have longed for is thus at hand, and I would doubtless be in high spirits were it not for the dream I dreamt last night.

I dreamt of Maria. I had not dreamt of her for some time and had begun to hope I was over it at last, but it seems not. In my dream I was a small child again and it was Maria's funeral day. The coffin had been lowered and I was looking into the grave, weeping bitterly. Everything was as I remember it, except that when my Aunt slipped her arm round me and began to lead me away, I looked back and saw myself sitting on the edge as if about to cast myself into the grave.

It was the opium I suppose, but I cannot keep from wondering whether the spirit of my dear sister knows I am going away, and is unhappy. Dreams and reality mingle so at times, a fellow can't tell which is which.

## NO EXCUSE

Tim had his elbows on the table and his head between his fists. He was staring at the copy of *Jane Eyre* which lay open before him. He'd been trying to read, but the print kept blurring and his eyelids smarted. Now his eyes were closed and he was thinking about a video they'd watched at home one night last winter. *The Shining*, with Jack Nicholson. Nicholson was snowed in with his wife and kid in this hotel in the mountains. Big, empty hotel, and a message kept appearing on a mirror, written in blood. REDRUM, it said. It was a sort of warning, only nobody knew what it meant. It was MURDER really, but it came out REDRUM because they were seeing it backwards in the mirror.

Look out. He opened his eyes and pretended to concentrate on the book as old Ellis approached. It was Ellis's habit to patrol the classroom, walking slowly with his hands behind his back, pausing here and there to peer at somebody's work over their shoulder. His footsteps stopped behind Tim. He leaned over. Tim could hear him breathing through his hairy nostrils.

'Question two, South? You're still on question two?' There were ten questions on the board, all to do with *Jane Eyre*.

Tim nodded. 'Yes, sir.'

'Why, lad? What have you been doing all this time? Some people have finished.'

'I was thinking, sir.'

'That's no excuse. What were you thinking about, South – your girlfriend, was it? Not *Jane Eyre*, I'll be bound.'

'He isn't going out with her, sir,' said a voice from a nearby table.

'That'll do, Cooper,' growled Ellis, and some of the kids sniggered. 'Well, South – what are these thoughts of yours? Share them with us.'

'I was thinking about mirrors, sir,' said Tim.

'Ah – you mean Brontë's mirror symbolism, as in Helen Burns as the mirror-image of Jane?'

'Yes, sir.' He hadn't the faintest idea what the man

49

was talking about, but it sounded good. The truth was that the red room in chapter two had reminded him of **REDRUM** and his mind had gone rambling on as usual. Still—.

'But that has nothing to do with question two, South. Question two asks "What evidence do we find in chapter three that Mrs. Reed does not regard Jane as a full member of her family?" Have you read chapter three, lad?'

'Yes, sir. I've read it through twice. I can't find it, sir.'

The teacher sighed. 'First page, paragraph three. And do promise me you'll buck up, South.'

Buck up. Oh sure. Easy. He'd been awake most of the night after that rotten dream, he was in the doghouse at home, and Chris and Alvin were looking up every time the door opened, expecting him to be summoned to the Head's office. Why the heck had he told them that stupid story? What were they going to say when no summons came? They'd never believe Dusty'd let him get away with it. He'd be exposed as a liar and a fraud.

And as if all that wasn't enough, there was the picture. It had lurked in the back of his mind ever since he found it, and it irritated him. Why couldn't he forget it for goodness sake – tear it up and chuck it away? Because I'm curious, he told himself. It's natural, isn't it? The man's my ancestor and nobody knows his name. He might have been famous. Fancy having a famous artist in the family and not knowing it. I just want to know who he was.

But why had he taken it out last night? What did it have to do with his dream? Nothing, as far as he could tell. And yet in the moment of waking, he must have fancied he saw a connection.

50

Dreams. He shook his head. They're nothing but a load of rubbish, right?

But then, what isn't?

## No Luck

He couldn't just sit around till it became obvious to everybody that the Head wasn't going to send for him. What he'd have to do was dodge everybody. It was the only way. When it got to three o'clock and old Hurford still hadn't sent for him, Chris and Alvin started giving him funny looks. Lee and Janis were in different groups most of the day Fridays, so he didn't see them once English was over. They'd be on to him at half past three as well, though, agog to know how he'd handled the Head. Given time he'd dream something up, of course – he'd have to, because even if he gave them all the slip today there was tomorrow night on the boat, and he wasn't going to miss that. I fantasized my way into this mess, he told himself, and I'll fantasize my way out of it, only not by half past three I won't. So. A dodge it will have to be.

Out front, a human skeleton dangled. Mrs Lightowler poked a stick at its grin. 'Mandible,' she intoned. 'Maxilla.'

He sure is, mused Tim. If that's Max, he couldn't hardly get no iller. He grinned to himself and went back to the problem of avoiding his friends. Five minutes before hometime he cracked it, putting up his hand and assuming an anxious, almost desperate expression.

51

'Yes, South, what is it?' Tim usually dreamed his way through biology and Mrs Lightowler didn't care for him much.

'Can I leave the room, Miss, please?'

She pursed her lips and made a big thing of looking at her watch. 'It's twenty-five past three, South. Couldn't you have waited just five minutes, instead of disrupting my lesson?'

'No, Miss. I've got this bug, Miss.'

'Bug?'

'Yes Miss. It's a tummy bug. A rare one. The doctor says –.'

Mrs Lightowler stopped him. 'I don't think we want to know the details, South. Off you go, and close the door behind you. Quietly.'

He hurried along to the lavatories and locked himself in a cubicle. Somebody had stuffed a comic behind the pipe. He sat and read it while the buzzer went and the kids came shouting and jostling along the corridors to get their coats. Doors banged and cisterns flushed as boys used other cubicles on the line. Once, somebody rattled his door and called out somebody else's name. He told whoever it was to naff off, and the noise gradually subsided till the place was silent. He waited five minutes longer in case they were hanging about near the gate. When he didn't show up they'd assume he'd slipped off before the buzzer.

He knew now exactly what he was going to do. This last minute excursion to the toilet had been a master stroke, enabling him to kill three birds with one stone. Not only had he avoided awkward questions, but he intended to claim that he'd been intercepted, hurrying back along the corridor in his desperate anxiety to rejoin the class, by somebody with a summons from the Head.

He'd tell them that's where he was while they were waiting for him outside school – in old Hurford's room, getting hell but sticking up for his rights. He smiled. The old imagination'd get him off the hook every time.

And since he'd broken his routine by leaving school late, he might as well pop down to the library in town and see if he could solve the mystery of his nameless ancestor. It was a fine afternoon and a bit of a walk would do him good.

At the library he asked for books on British painters of the nineteenth century. An assistant pulled out about ten fat volumes and he lugged them to a table and started going through them, looking for pictures of the artists themselves. There weren't many, and none of those he found looked anything like the man in the picture at home. He was riffling through the last tome when somebody touched him on the shoulder. He looked round and found Dilys grinning down at him.

'Oh hi, Dil.' Her words of the day before were raw in his memory, and he neither smiled nor put too much enthusiasm into his greeting, but she seemed not to notice.

'What you doing?' she hissed, looking at the pile of books. 'I didn't know you were into this sort of stuff.'

'I'm not, only I found this picture in our attic.' Amazing, he thought. One day she makes me hate her guts and the next I'm trotting at her heel like a flaming poodle. He started to tell her about the portrait but somebody went, 'Sssh!'

'Oh, hush yourself,' he muttered, without looking to see who it was. 'Come on – I'll tell you in the coffee bar.'

The library had its own coffee bar. They got cokes and sat at one of the little plastic tables. Most of the other customers were down-and-outs in layers of grubby clothing, who stared vacantly at the wall or into empty teacups.

Dilys sucked up some coke and looked at Tim. 'What were you saying?'

He told her about the picture – how he'd found it, what his gran had said and how he couldn't stop thinking about it. 'I thought if he became an artist he might be in a book somewhere, even if he wasn't all that famous, so I came down here.'

'And?'

He shrugged. 'No luck. There must have been hundreds of painters in those days. Without a name, it's like looking for a needle in a haystack.'

'Have you got the picture on you?'

He shook his head. 'I didn't know I was coming, did I? Why are you here, anyway?'

'I came for this.' She opened her sport bag and pulled out a thin volume.

'What is it?'

'Guide to *Jane Eyre*. I thought I'd have a look at the sorts of questions we might get in the exam.'

He snorted. 'Trust you to be doing something useful. All I can think about is that stupid picture.'

'Well, you'll have to stop thinking about it, won't you? Put it out of your mind, Tim. It's not long to the exams, you know.'

'You don't have to tell me. Are you off on this trip?'

'The Haworth trip? Yes, I'm going. Wouldn't miss it for anything. Are you?'

'I suppose so. Chris and them are going. It's a few days out of school if nothing else.'

She looked at him. 'It'll be nothing else if you tag

along with that lot. I wouldn't even take them if I was Mr Ellis.'

'Well, you're not. Anyway, I like them, and it's not just because they laugh at my jokes, either.'

Instead of replying she stood up. 'I'd better get off. What you doing tomorrow?'

'I'm off out around seven. Why?'

'I meant in the afternoon. You could come over. Mum and Dad'll be at my gran's. We could play records or something. What d'you reckon?'

'I dunno.'

'Well, don't strain yourself, only I'll be in if you feel like calling round. See you.'

Tim nodded and stayed where he was, sipping coke and watching the down-and-outs. After a while one of them, a thin man with grey skin and red-rimmed eyes, began to shout. He wasn't shouting at anybody in particular, but his pale blue eyes darted about the room and he was trembling, apparently with indignation.

''S all right for them!' he cried, and when nobody responded he repeated the phrase more loudly. 'I said it's all right for them.' He stared madly about him as though defying anybody to contradict. His fellow unfortunates ignored him, but his ranting was making the other customers uncomfortable. They looked out of the window, or conversed doggedly with rigid faces, or drained their cups and gathered up their belongings. Tim sat and stared, which was a mistake because the man caught his eye and began shouting directly at him.

'Oh, aye!' He shook his small skull with its wisps of grey-white hair. 'They're all right. Their bread's buttered, innit? Innit, eh?'

Tim felt as if every eye in the place was on him. The man seemed to want his agreement so he nodded and

55

grinned in what he hoped was a friendly way, thinking he'd be satisfied and shut up.

He didn't. Tim's response encouraged him and he leaned towards him, shouting even louder. 'Buttered, that's what their bread is. Buttered. Buttered, buttered, buttered, buttered, buttered, buttered, buttered!' Spittle sprayed from his mouth and he pounded the table with his fist so that the cup and saucer on it rattled and jumped.

Tim had had enough. People were staring. If he stayed where he was they'd think he knew the guy or something. He shoved back his chair, stood up and hurried out with flaming cheeks, praying that the demented fellow wouldn't follow.

He didn't, but he'd got inside Tim's skull and so Tim had to carry him about, and see his face whenever he closed his eyes.

## PURE MUCK

Saturday morning there was a postcard from Rebecca, who was touring in Spain with a fellow student. It was a panoramic view across the city of Toledo – a chequerboard pattern of glare and deep shadow under an impossibly perfect sky. Scrawled on the reverse was the message 'The weather's here – wish you were beautiful.'

'Cheeky monkey!' said Tim's mother, passing the card to her husband across the breakfast table. 'Just look what she's put. You'd think when she's gone gallivanting off abroad instead of coming home, the least she could do would be to write something nice.'

Mr South read the message and chuckled. 'It's only a bit of fun, Liz. She's a kid, and that's how kids are. Besides, it's quite clever in a way – inversion of a hackneyed and totally silly message. I mean, who really wishes their relatives were with them when they're away on holiday? Nobody, that's who. The whole point of going off is to get away from relatives.'

'It's out of a song,' growled Tim, placing his empty eggshell upside down in the egg-cup and smashing the top in with his spoon. His mother shot him a look which was both enquiring and disapproving.

'What d'you say, dear?'

'It's a song. "The Weather's Here, Wish You Were Beautiful.' Country and Western singer, can't remember his name.' He didn't see why his sister should get the credit for somebody else's clever line.

'Oh, is it? Well, I'm not surprised. They have such awful lyrics nowadays – rude, suggestive stuff, most of it. Pure muck. And how many times have I asked you not to do that?' She nodded towards the ruined eggshell. 'It means I have to fish out all those little bits before I can start the washing up.'

'He hasn't grown up, Liz, that's his trouble.' Her husband spoke as if Tim wasn't there. 'Never will, if you ask me. Look at that business at school the other day. It's high time he started acting his age.'

'You just said Becky was a kid,' Tim protested, 'and she's four years older than me. If it's all right for her to act daft, why isn't it all right for me?'

His father put the postcard down and looked at him. 'Your sister has always behaved sensibly where it really matters, Tim. When she needed three A levels at grade

57

one to get into medical school she sat and studied, night after night. And she got them. If that had been you, you'd have been off every night with that bunch of deadeyes you call friends, and then you'd have been aggrieved when the qualifications didn't fall into your lap. Rebecca's on her way, lad. She can afford a bit of tomfoolery now and again. She's earned it, you haven't. So if you're not going to buckle down and work, the least you can do is behave.'

'Well,' Tim told himself later, polishing up his bike in the late April sunshine, 'with a gorgeous start like that, the weekend can only get better.'

He was wrong.

## GOING OUT

There was no car on the drive when Tim got to Dilys's house around two. Good. He suspected her parents weren't too crazy about him, and anyway he preferred to have her to himself. He grinned and pounded on the door so hard with the side of his fist it nearly fell off its hinges. When he heard footsteps in the hallway he thrust his hand through the letter slot and wiggled his fingers.

The door was opened by a lad of about nineteen. He was easily six feet tall, and it was obvious from his expression that he'd half expected to find a dangerous lunatic on the step.

'Yes?'

Tim felt his face go red. He wanted to run. Who the heck's this? he thought. I must have the wrong house.

He grinned sheepishly and stammered, 'Oh, s-sorry – I was looking for the Williams's place.'

'I'm Gerald Williams. Can I help at all?'

Of course! Dil had a brother Becky's age. At university. He'd forgotten.

'I – I'm a friend of Dilys's.'

'Oh, right – she said she was expecting somebody.' He turned and called into the house. 'Dil – it's for you.' He looked at Tim. 'Won't you come in?'

'Thanks.' Tim stepped over the threshold and the lad closed the door.

'She'll be down in a minute,' he said, and went off.

Tim looked round. The hallway was nearly as big as his parents' house and was very old-fashioned, with tiles on the floor and walls done in brown and dark green. The only light came from a narrow window beside the door and from the fanlight above it, and since both these were of heavily leaded stained glass the effect was one of almost subterranean gloom. There was a hallstand with coats, umbrellas and walking sticks and a small black table with an aspidistra in a green pot. On the wall was an oval mirror in a rich gilt frame. It's like a flippin' museum, thought Tim. How we used to live.

He caught sight of his reflection in the mirror and noticed that he looked dishevelled. The light was poor and he had no comb so he went right up to the mirror and lifted his hand to run his fingers through his hair. *There was nothing wrong with his hair.* His palm brushed over stiffish spikes, every one in place. Fear stabbed his gut and he stepped back quickly, gazing at the image in the glass, seeing the hand half buried in a frizzy mane.

It was then he heard footfalls on the stair and turned. Dilys came down smiling. 'Hi, Tim. I didn't know

59

whether you'd show up.' She noticed his expression. 'What's wrong?'

He shook his head. 'Nothing.' He couldn't say anything. She'd think he was barmy, like the old guy at the library. *He* was barmy all right. Well off his trolley, that one. He risked a glance at the mirror but couldn't make out details. Dilys smiled.

'Where's Gerry?' Tim nodded along the hallway.

'He went that way.'

'Typical, the ignorant pig. Leaving you standing there. Come on – I'll introduce you.'

I introduced myself, he thought miserably, following her. Tim South, the human battering-ram and well-known headcase. Why isn't Gerry touring Spain or something? Why did I look in that mirror?

Dilys led him through to the kitchen, where Gerry was doing something technical to an electric kettle. He looked up as the pair came in.

'Tim,' said Dilys. 'This is my brother Gerry who used to torture me when I was little. Gerry, meet Tim.'

Tim grinned awkwardly and stuck out the hand he'd posted through the slot. As he did so he remembered something about reflections. As the older boy put down the kettle and took his hand, Tim said, 'When you stand in front of a mirror and raise your right hand, your reflection raises its left.'

Gerry released Tim's hand and grinned at his sister. 'You didn't tell me your friend was a genius, Dil.'

Tim flushed, and Dilys laughed. 'Stop embarrassing him, Gerry, he's the shy type.'

'He doesn't have a shy knock, Dil.' He looked at Tim. 'Schoolmates, are you – you and Dil?'

'Yes, that's right. We have some classes together. English. A few others.'

60

'So you're doing *Jane Eyre* too?'

'Right.'

'Great novel. Charlotte Brontë's employment of the pathetic fallacy is tremendously effective, don't you think?'

'Ooh, not half!' He hadn't the faintest idea what the lad was talking about, and he suspected that both Gerry and Dilys knew this. If he hadn't been blushing already he would certainly have done so now.

'Take no notice of him, Tim,' said Dilys. 'He's showing off. People are supposed to grow up a bit at university, but that's another pathetic fallacy.' She grinned. 'Come on. We'll go upstairs and you can thrash me at table tennis.'

As they left the kitchen Gerry called after them. 'You'll have no trouble there, Tim. My little sister doesn't play table tennis, she plays ping-pong.'

The Williams' house had three attics, two of them full size rooms in which servants had once slept. One of these had been fitted out as a games room. As they climbed the stairs Dilys said, 'What was all that about reflections, Tim?'

Tim shrugged. 'Nothing.'

'It's a funny thing to say when you're being introduced to somebody. Gerry'll think I've taken up with some kind of nut.'

'Will he? I hope not, Dil. It was something I was thinking about, that's all.'

They played. An hour went by. Dilys wasn't a bad player – certainly not the ping-pong artist her brother had accused her of being, but Tim was on the point of beating her by two sets to one when the stairs creaked and Gerry sauntered in with his hands in his pockets, causing Tim to tense up and lose the point. 'Seven –

twenty,' called Dilys, as he bent to retrieve the ball. 'Here I come.'

'What's the state of the match?' asked Gerry.

His sister wiped her forehead with the back of her hand. 'It's the final game, third set,' she told him. 'Tim won the first set, I took the second and it's one game all in this set. We're at seven – twenty, my serve, so Tim needs one point for the match. Come on, Tim.'

Tim tossed the ball to her and she served. Tim, aware of Gerry watching, overhit the return, sending the ball soaring above his opponent's head. 'Eight – twenty!' she laughed, turning to fetch it. 'Watch your sister snatch victory from the jaws of defeat, Gerry.'

It was never going to happen. Although Tim's game had fallen apart under Gerry's mild gaze his lead was unassailable. Dilys took the next two points, but then, with the change of service, Tim served an unplayable ball to clinch the match.

'Well played,' panted Dilys.

'Hard luck,' grinned Tim.

'I'll play the winner,' said Gerry.

The two boys played. Dilys kept score. Gerry was cool and efficient. Tim was clumsy and flustered. He fell over twice and hit himself on the side of the head with his bat, knocking his glasses off and making Dilys laugh. In three sets he managed a grand total of eleven points. When the massacre was over, it was as much as he could do to keep from bursting into tears of humiliation.

Gerry was magnanimous in victory. 'Thanks for the game,' he said. 'You're not bad, actually.' He hadn't even broken sweat.

'Poor old Tim,' soothed Dilys, when her brother had

gone downstairs. 'You didn't play nearly as well as you can, y'know.'

Tim pulled a face. 'I know. I fall apart round people I don't know, Dil. I always assume they're going to be better than me for some reason. I can't help it.'

Dilys was seeing him off at the gate when the family car drew up. Mrs Williams beamed at her daughter and said, 'Would your friend like to stay for tea, dear?'

No, thanks, thought Tim. I've enjoyed myself enough for one day. He forced a smile. 'I can't, Mrs Williams, thanks all the same. I'm going out.' He smiled at Dilys. 'See you Monday, okay?'

Pedalling home, he thought about the mirror. He remembered how messy his hair had looked and how neat it had felt and how, when he'd raised his right hand to straighten it, his reflection had raised its right hand, too.


# TIMMO'S SHOUT


Tim had tea at home, watched the end of Grandstand and then left the house, telling his parents he was off for a walk. He was on edge. He'd brooded all day over his poor showing against Gerry, and the mirror thing had bothered him, too. He needed to feel ten feet tall again, but time seemed to be standing still. He went to Linley Park to kill some of it. It was a dry evening, cloudy but quite warm, and he sat on a bench by the lake, looking at the ducks. There was a woman on the next bench, watching her toddler throw bread in the water. There were some ducklings and the kid was trying to feed them but her throwing was erratic and the ducklings weren't quick enough. Every time a piece of bread hit the water some big bird would dart in and scoop it up. The kid was becoming more and more frustrated and, as he watched her, Tim thought: she doesn't know it, but she's raging against the unfairness little people find in a big people's world. The lake's the same as everywhere else. Big people show up and spoil everything.

Tim nodded and smiled to himself, surprised and pleased at this insight. He thought he might even do a bit about it for old Ellis in creative writing. It was the sort of thing he'd lap up – the sort of thing he was forever finding in the novels they read in class.

Presently the kid burst into tears. The woman went over, picked her up and carried her away, making soothing noises as she went. Tim looked at his watch. Twenty-five past six. If he dawdled a bit he could set off now towards the hulk. The incredible hulk. There'd be nobody there yet, of course, but there might be by the time he got there.

As he got up he noticed that the bag which the kid had dropped still had a crust in it. He picked it up. The birds saw him and turned, converging on his bit of bank. He waited till the ducklings were close, then threw half the crust far off to his left. The adult birds sped after it leaving the little ones to bob cheeping in their wake. Time crumbled the half crust and lobbed the fragments into their midst. They snatched up the food, threw their heads back and guzzled. Tim watched for a moment, then headed for the gate. Passing a litter basket he balled up the paper bag and dropped it in. He felt good, and left the park whistling.

He got to the hulk just after seven. There was nobody

there. He sat in the bow with his legs over the side, dabbling the soles of his trainers in the water and watching people go by on the far bank. Some glanced across as they passed, others didn't notice him under the tender spring foliage.

He was working up a good story about his supposed interview with the Head yesterday, when two boys of about his own age came along. One of them spotted Tim and plucked at his companion's sleeve, pointing. Tim waved and said, 'Hi.' The boys waved back, and one of them called out 'What you doing?'

Tim shrugged. 'Sitting.'

'Whose boat is it?'

'Mine. Well, my dad's, really, but he's finished with it.'

'Can we come over?'

'I wouldn't. He's touchy about his property, my dad.'

'But if he's finished with it—.'

'Makes no difference. Once, when I was little, he threw an old coat in the dustbin. A few days later he went down town, saw a guy wearing it and damn near killed him.'

'He must be some sort of nut, your dad.'

'He got this head wound in Nam. Not been right since.'

'The British weren't in Nam.'

'No. He's an Aussie, my dad.'

'How come you don't talk like an Aussie, then?'

'My dad was away all the time. My mum brought me up. She's English.'

'Did he go to Nam by barge, or what?'

'Yeah. Sailed up the Mekong, destroyed a guerrilla base and got shot up on the way back. They hit him in

65

the head and holed the barge. Only just made it here before it sank.'

'Huh! I don't think it's your dad's boat at all. We're coming over.'

'I wouldn't be you, then.'

The pair went on, passing from sight round the bend. Tim stood up. Phil and the others wouldn't be too pleased if they arrived to find strangers on board, but there were two of them, and they were both bigger than he was. He looked around for something to use as a weapon.

He found it as the boys came in sight, picking their way through the undergrowth. It was an old broom which had been used for spreading pitch. Its head was just a black heavy lump, stuck to some rotten planking. He wrenched it free and stood brandishing it.

The two boys looked at him. 'Who d'you think you are?' sneered one. 'Captain Bligh?'

'Captain Pugwash, more like,' said the other. 'Rush him, Ronnie.'

'Hang on,' protested Ronnie. 'I don't want to end up in the water.' He looked at Tim. 'There's two of us,' he pointed out. 'And we only want to look round.'

'Naff off,' said Tim.

Ronnie smiled. 'Okay, Ginger,' he said. 'You've had your chance. Daz – go on there a bit, and when I say jump, jump.'

Daz was moving to obey when there were sounds of movement in the undergrowth and Phil Barraclough appeared, followed closely by Chris and the others. They stood, the five of them, looking at Daz and Ronnie.

'It's Tweedledum and Tweedle-flippin'-dee,' growled Phil. 'Looking for a scrap, are you?'

'N-no,' said Ronnie innocently. 'We were just talking

to your mate here, weren't we, Daz?'

'Yeah. Showing us his brush, he was.'

'Oh, aye? Well, you've seen it now, haven't you, so you'd better be on your way, unless you want me to show you how far down your gullet I can get it.'

Anxious to avoid such a demonstration, the pair hurried away through the trees. Tim put the broom where he'd found it as the others leapt aboard. 'Good old Prof!' cried Phil, ruffling Tim's hair. 'Stood by to repel boarders, he did, all five foot naff-all of him. I bet he'll give old Hurford hell and all, when he sends for him. Give him a beer, somebody.'

Alvin had some sixpacks in a plastic carrier. He split one and they sat in a line along the bow, drinking from cans while Tim told them about the Hurford interview. It was a good story – one of the best he'd ever dreamed up – and it seemed to go down well with the beer. Tim had never tasted beer before. He didn't like it much but he didn't say so. He felt happy. There was a glow inside. He was Good old Prof, right? A fully paid-up member, basking in the group's approval, and Dil's obnoxious brother was a million miles away.

As the sun sank and the shadows lengthened, Phil produced the makings and rolled a couple of joints. When Janis passed the first of these to him, Tim said, 'Where d'you get this stuff, anyway?'

Phil chuckled. 'We thought you'd never ask, Prof, old lad. We buy it. Twelve quid an eighth. We take it in turns. It's your turn next, as it happens.'

'My turn?' Tim's stomach lurched. 'But, I don't know anything about it. I mean, where to get it or anything.'

'You've smoked ours, though, haven't you?' Phil appealed to the others. 'What d'you say, you lot – Timmo's shout next, or what?'

'Oh, definitely.' They grinned and nodded. 'Definitely Timmo's shout. He's supped our ale and all.'

Tim shrugged, forcing a grin. 'Okay. That's fair enough. I don't mind paying my corner, but our offie won't sell beer to kids my age, and I've no idea where to get – the other stuff.'

'You don't need to,' Phil told him. 'You bring the brass and I'll score, right? Twelve quid. I'll even fetch the ale for you. Now I can't say fairer than that, can I?'

Tim was forced to agree, but a cloud settled over his evening which neither beer nor smoking could quite disperse.

# OF BOOKS AND OF BATTLES

It is late. I am in my room and the house is silent. In two days I shall leave this place and nothing, for me, will ever be the same. I had thought that by now I might be in the grip of an anticipation so eager as to render me irrepressibly happy, but it is not so. Events and persons still have the power to depress my spirit, as I learned to my cost today.

There was an outing, to the ruins at Bolton Priory. Ellen and Emily had got it up between them as a sort of farewell gift to me. Ellen had hired a two-wheeled gig, and I was to be in charge of the horse. It was a kindly, if extravagant gesture on their part, and I might have enjoyed the day immensely had it not been for the fact that in the party were two cousins of ours – puffed-up young men from Bradford who spent the entire day airing their knowledge in a palpable bid to impress the ladies and to make me seem a clod by comparison. They prattled throughout the two-and-a-half hour journey, talking of books and of battles; and at the priory, strutted and swaggered and preened like peacocks till it was time to come home. Both are tall young men whom some might consider handsome, and are I suppose educated, in a shallow sort of way. Needless to say, the ladies' response to their ridiculous behaviour was such as not to disappoint them, and this encouraged them to a degree where a fellow could scarcely get a word in. At Ellen's suggestion, for the return journey one of them took the reins; and I sat silent as a sack of potatoes, the whole fourteen miles. Thus, an event which had been intended to cheer and divert me, cast me down instead.

I have my bottle now, and with its help am endeavouring to look on the bright side, thus: had today's excursion proved a joyous occasion for me, I might have begun to regret my imminent parting from those who planned it. As it is, my cousins spoiled the day, and my consolation lies in the fact that soon I shall leave them far behind and go to London, where such fellows, I am sure, do not exist.


# YOUR PIGGY-BANK RATTLES

Sunday morning Tim woke up feeling bad. He'd drunk two tinnies, smoked quite a bit and had rotten dreams all night. His eyes burned, his head hurt every time he moved it and his mouth tasted like the inside of an angler's maggot-tin.

It was a sunny morning. Downstairs, his mother sang as she drew back the curtains and started breakfast. His father backed the car out of the garage and set to work with hose and wax and chammy. Tim lay on his back with his eyes closed, wincing at their noise.

Presently the fumes inside his skull began to clear and he remembered he was supposed to find twelve pounds. He'd promised to meet Chris this morning at the café in Lindley Park with the cash. He rolled on his side and opened his eyes a slit to peer at the clock-radio. Light lasered his brain and he fell back, groaning. Twenty past nine. What time had Chris said? Ten, was it? Half past? If it was ten there was no chance. If it was half past, well maybe.

He had the money. Three fivers, in the piggy-bank on his bookshelf. His auntie Pam had given him the piggy-bank on his fourth birthday and he loved it. China, it was. White, with a slick glaze and big pink daisies. His mates'd laugh if they found out he still used a piggy-bank, but they weren't going to find out. All his spare change went in that pig, and when there was a fiver's worth he swapped it for a note, unscrewing the cap in the pig's belly and cramming the fiver in. His emergency money, he called it. Cash he could draw on if he saw something he fancied in a shop. His real savings – the five pounds his dad put away for him each week in the building society – were practically untouchable. The money was supposed to be for when he got married or something. It went in the building society because his dad was Assistant Manager there, and it might as well be in Fort Knox.

He had the piggy-bank cash all right, but he'd had

plans for it as well. He'd intended taking it with him on the Haworth trip. An extra fifteen quid, in case it got boring and there were things a guy with money could do. It had taken him ages to get it together, and now there'd only be three pounds left, and no more than a couple of weeks before the trip.

Well, he told himself, it's too late to worry about that now. I'd better shake off this hangover or whatever, and get myself down Linley Park, pronto.

In the bathroom, he filled the basin with cold water and ducked his head. It was what guys with hangovers did in the movies and it always seemed to fix them up fine, but it didn't make him feel much better. He pulled on jeans and a sweatshirt, dragged a comb across his sodden head and went downstairs. His parents were eating scrambled eggs and bacon.

'Good morning, Tim.'

'Morning, Mum.'

'Your plate's in the microwave, love. Half a minute'll be long enough.' She looked at him. 'Are you feeling all right?'

He nodded, which was a mistake, because the sliding brick which had replaced his brain hit him behind the eyes and then rebounded, slamming into the back of his skull. 'I'm okay, Mum, but I'm not hungry. I feel like a breath of fresh air.'

His father lowered the newspaper and gave him a baleful stare. 'You don't look like a breath of fresh air,' he growled. 'What were you doing last night?'

Tim shrugged. 'Sitting by the canal, talking.'

'To whom?'

'To my mates, Dad. Chris and Janis and them.'

'Was Phillip Barraclough there?'

'Yes.'

'Did he take you all to the pub?'

'Pub? I'm fifteen, Dad. They wouldn't even let me in a pub.'

'He's had young Christopher in one. They were seen. I don't ever want to hear of you being seen in one, Tim.'

'You won't. Can I get that fresh air now, please?'

It was five past ten when he got to the park, ten past when he walked into the café. Chris and Lee were eating bacon butties and drinking Coke. Fat Hilda was fussing about behind the counter in her greasy overall, and the only other customer was an old man with a dog. The dog's leash was tied to the old man's chair. As Tim came in the animal, a Jack Russell, jumped up and capered about on the end of its leash, whining. The old man reeled it in and cuffed its head.

'Afternoon, Prof,' greeted Lee, through a mouthful of butty. 'You're late.'

'Am I heck. You said half past and it's only ten past.'

'Ten o'clock,' contradicted Chris. 'It was supposed to be ten o'clock. Got the brass, have you?'

'Course.'

'That's all right, then. Get a butty and a drink and sit down.'

'Ugh! No way. Hang on and I'll get a coffee.'

Hilda poured coffee into a thick white cup and plonked it on the counter. Some of the coffee slopped in the saucer. 'Thirty pence.' She didn't smile or say please. She didn't like young people much. She liked them even less when Tim offered a five pound note.

'You got owt smaller?'

He shook his head. 'Sorry.' He had, but he wanted the fiver split so he could give Chris twelve.

Lee twisted round in his chair. 'He has got summat smaller, love – his brain.'

Hilda didn't smile. She snatched the note and made a big thing out of rummaging in the till, muttering something which sounded like 'All my change. All my bleedin' change.' She came up with a load of old iron – tens, fives and coppers – which she dumped in Tim's cupped hands.

He carried it across the café, spilled it on the table and counted out two pounds' worth, which he pushed across to Chris with his precious fivers. All that money, he grieved. And for what? An eighth of an ounce of resin. Jeez – an eighth of an ounce!

'There y'are,' he grunted. 'Twelve. When do we get together?' He'd just done all his savings. He wanted to be sure he'd be there to share the meagre purchase.

Chris scooped up the cash and dropped it in his pocket. 'Wednesday, Phil said. He scores Tuesday night. Wednesday, around seven. He'll need something for beer as well.'

Tim swallowed. 'From me?'

'Sure, from you. You drank Alvin's last night, didn't you?'

Beer, it turned out, was £3.60 a sixpack. Tim had £2.70 left out of his fifteen pounds, plus two pounds odd he'd had in his pocket. When he left the café, alone, fifteen minutes later he had exactly forty-four pence to his name – thirty on him and fourteen in the china pig – and there'd be no pocket money till Saturday.

Lee's dead right, he thought bitterly, going round by the pond to see if the ducklings had a crust for him. I have got a tiny brain. I must have.

And that wasn't all. When he got home his mother said. 'I cleaned your room this morning, Tim.'

'Thanks,' he said.

73

'I'm not fishing for thanks,' she told him. 'But when I dust I move things, and your piggy bank rattles. It didn't rattle before because it was too full of notes. What have you done with the notes, Tim?'

## OLD HORSES

'Where's Dad?' asked Tim. He needed a story, and stories need time.

'Down at Charlie Brown's buying wiper-blades,' his mother told him. 'It's what *you've* been buying that bothers me. There must have been at least ten pounds in that pig.'

'Fifteen,' said Tim. 'And I haven't been buying anything.'

'Then where's the money, Tim?'

'I gave it away.'

'What? Fifteen pounds? Why? Who've you given it to? Are you in some sort of trouble, Tim?'

Tim shook his head. 'No, Mum. No trouble. It's gone to a home for old horses.'

'Old—?' His mother looked at him. 'What home for old horses? Where?'

Tim shrugged. 'I don't know where, do I? There's this girl. At school. Mad on horses. Works weekends at this home for old ones. It used to be a farm. She doesn't get paid or anything. She was collecting and I felt like helping, you know?'

'Helping? Helping's one thing, Tim. Throwing away fifteen pounds is quite another. I mean, by all means give a few pence. A couple of pounds, even. But fifteen. Are you keen on this girl or something? Is that it? What's her name?'

'Janis. And no, I'm not keen on her, as you call it. I felt sorry for the old horses, that's all.'

'Janis? She's one of Christopher Barraclough's friends, isn't she? I can't imagine a girl like that caring about old horses.'

Tim shook his head. 'Not that Janis, Mum. You're thinking of Janis Clegg. It's Janis Joplin who looks after the horses.'

'Janis Joplin?' His mother frowned. 'She was a singer, wasn't she? Died of drugs or something. Are you sure you're not making all this up, Tim?'

'Course I'm sure. I know the difference between fact and fiction, don't I? Her folks called her after the singer. They were fans, see? When they were young.'

'Ah.'

'Anyway, it was my money, Mum. I saved it. I can do what I like with my own money, can't I?'

There was sadness in his mother's eyes, and a catch in her voice when she spoke. 'Well, yes, of course you can Tim, and it's a very generous thing you've done. A very kind gesture. I can think of far worse things a boy your age might do with fifteen pounds.' She gave him a watery smile, reached out and hugged him briefly. 'You're a good boy, Tim, and there's nothing wrong with being generous, but it is possible sometimes to be over generous, and I think you might have been just a little bit over generous towards the old horses, don't you?'

He shrugged. 'Maybe.' He was looking at the floor because he couldn't meet his mother's eye. He wished he hadn't told her the story. He wished he still had his

75

money. He wished he *had* given it to a home for old horses.

'Hey listen, Mum. Dad doesn't need to know, does he?'

'Well – no, I suppose not. Not if you don't want him to, Tim.' She smiled. 'I daresay he'd be a bit upset at first, but deep down he'd be as proud of you as I am.'

Tim's cheeks burned with shame. His mother took the flush for modesty and ruffled his hair. 'Go on with you,' she smiled. 'Out from under my feet. Some of us have work to do.'

He fled to the attic and sat with his head in his hands, torturing himself with futile regrets. In a shadowy corner stood Silver, the only old horse he knew.

## OTHER SOURCES

'Bit of good stuff, this.' Phil took the cigarette from Lee and studied it drowsily before placing it between his lips. He took a long drag and closed his eyes, holding the smoke in his lungs before exhaling a languid plume and passing the cigarette to his brother.

He was stoned, and a bit drunk. They all were. He'd added some money of his own to Tim's contribution and they'd got through three sixpacks since seven o'clock. Now the empties bobbed unseen on the black water inside the hulk, and the light was almost gone.

'It ought to be good,' slurred Tim. 'It cost enough.' Adrift on a narcotic sea, he was still aware of his sorrow bobbing like an empty on the surface.

Phil regarded him through half-closed eyes. 'Shurrup moaning, you miserable little prat. You've paid your corner, that's all, same as everybody else. No need to keep on about it.'

'I'm not moaning, and I'm not keeping on. All I said was it ought to be good.'

'Yeah, well it is, only it isn't doing you much good because you're nattering yourself about the brass all the time. The brass has gone, kid. Forget it. Let go, like there's plenty more where that came from.'

Tim chuckled mirthlessly. 'There's fourteen pence where that came from. Fourteen pence to last me five days at Haworth. That's why I'm finding it hard to let go, Phil.'

'Your folks'll see you right, and if they don't, there's always other sources.'

'How d'you mean, other sources? I've got no other sources.'

'Course you have. Everybody has, if they know where to look. How d'you think I manage? And them?' He jerked his head towards the others. 'They don't have dads with posh jobs like you have, but they get by.'

'Yes, but how?'

Phil chuckled. 'Tell him, Chris.'

Chris passed the cigarettes to Janis and gazed at Tim across the hatchway, 'You've got a gran, right?'

Tim nodded. 'Sure, but she's a pensioner. I can't ask her for money.'

'Nobody said owt about asking.' He leaned forward. 'Listen. Old people, right? They don't bank their cash, do they? They have a drawer or something, or else they stick it under the mattress. And your gran's old, isn't she? Get it?'

Tim stared at his friend. 'You mean I should rob her?

77

My own gran? Is that what—.'

He glanced around. They were all looking at him. He saw amusement in their eyes. Alvin grinned and nodded, and Janis said 'What good's it to them, eh? They don't buy owt or go anywhere. They hoard it, that's all. Most of 'em don't even know how much they've got. Then they die and it all goes to the cats' home or the government or somewhere.'

Tim shook his head. 'I couldn't do it. No way. It's horrible.'

Phil laughed. 'What's up, Prof – don't you know where she keeps it?'

'Course I do. It's in her bedroom drawer, but it's hers. I'd rather be broke forever than steal from my gran.'

'Okay, okay.' Tim's voice had risen and Phil held up his hands, palms outward. 'Nobody's asking you to rob your gran, Prof. All we're saying is, there's bags of brass about if you know where to look.'

Nobody mentioned the subject again. They sat, smoking the last of the cigarettes and watching the stars come out, and by the time they separated around ten o'clock Tim had worked out a way to solve his financial problem without stealing from his gran. He'd borrow from her. If you borrow something, intending to return it, then even if the person you're borrowing from doesn't know about it, it's not stealing, is it?'

Is it heck.

# SWEET GOLDEN CLIME

What a journey. So shaken up have I been these two days by the swaying and jolting of the coach that when, having been shown to my room and flung myself for weariness on the bed, it seemed to move on twisted wheels along a rutted track. Even now, after two hours and with a good dinner inside me I dare not close my eyes, lest my bed propel its guest I know not whither!

Ah, but I find myself at last in London:

> ... *that sweet golden clime,*
> *Where the traveller's journey is done.*

Our lodging disappoints me. The Chapter Coffee House, Paternoster Row. My father lodged here often in his youth, and its name and location have always conjured in my mind's eye a vision of some awesome edifice exuding dignity: a place steeped in the erudition and the wit of its famous former patrons: in short, a venerable repository of culture.

In fact the place is dingy. It has seen better days, without having retained anything of their flavour. I said as much to Robinson, who saw fit to reply that my judgement was hasty, my disappointment premature. He is wrong. The place reeks of dust. Its rooms and corridors echo the arid scratchings, the furtive scurryings of dry provincial clerics. I can see my father here, but not Doctor Johnson.

The view from my window likewise fails to inspire. Rooftops. Reeking chimneys. Little streets all cramped and mean. One finds such views in Bradford. Where are the towers and the palaces, majestic river, gleaming domes?

Tomorrow. It is late and I am tired, but somewhere beyond this grimy pane, waiting for me, lies my Verdopolis: city of my dreams and of my destiny. It has waited always, and now the time is nigh. Tomorrow I shall find it at last.

Tomorrow.

# BORROWING TIME

Saturday, April 30th. Nine days to Haworth, fourteen pence in the piggy bank, action time. At breakfast, Tim said, 'I thought I'd pop over to Grandma's this morning, Mum. Is there anything you'd like me to take?'

His mother smiled. 'That's considerate of you, Tim. Yes, you can take her my love. Oh, and this. She'd like to see this, I'm sure.'

'This' was a postcard which had arrived that morning from Becky. It was a view of the university. On the back she'd written:

'Safe back from Spain
Rain.
Working again
Pain.'

'Okay.' He slipped the postcard in his pocket and stood up.

His father said, 'What's come over you all of a sudden, Tim? Your mother's practically had to beg you to visit your grandma in the past, and now you're off before your breakfast's settled.'

'Yeah, well.' Tim shrugged. 'She's on her own, isn't she? It must get a bit of a drag, cooped up in Celandine House. I'll see you.'

It was drizzling outside. He zipped his jacket, turned the collar up and set off along Anemone Way with his hands in his pockets and his head down. He hadn't wanted to hang about in case his mother took it into her head to come with him. The last thing he needed on this trip was company.

His grandma answered the door with her coat on and a shopping bag over her arm with an umbrella sticking out of it. She seemed surprised to see him. 'Oh, hello, Tim. I was just off to do my bit of shopping. Come on in.'

Tim grinned. 'I've got a better idea. Give me your list and your bag, and I'll get your shopping for you.'

She shook her head. 'You're wet through, lad. I can't have you traipsing about in the rain without a coat on. And, anyway, I haven't got a list, and I'm going with Mrs. Pearson next door. We always go together – it's the only bit of fresh air and exercise we get. Come on in.'

She put her bag down, led him into the living room and lit the gas fire. 'There. Take that jacket off and let me hang it on the radiator. Sit and dry your trousers while I'm gone. I shan't be long; then we'll have a cup of tea and a chat.'

She went off. Tim hadn't expected the place to himself – hadn't expected it to be so easy. He sat in the chair and gazed into the fire, struggling to steady himself.

It's April 30th, right? And I need fifteen quid. On

June 26th it's my birthday and I'll have fifteen quid, won't I? More. So I don't need the money – that's on its way. What I need is time – seven weeks. So if I take fifteen quid now and put it back on my birthday, I'm not pinching money, am I? I'm not even borrowing money, really. I'm borrowing time.

It wasn't one of his better stories, but the old lady might return any minute and so it would have to do. He got up and went out to the bedroom. It smelled of lavender. A board creaked as he crossed to the dressing table. Top right hand drawer, if he remembered correctly. He eased it open. In the mirror, his image did the same and Tim avoided its eyes. He peered into the drawer, lifting things.

A wad of brown envelopes held together by a rubber band. An old wallet full of black and white snapshots. Some documents – insurance or something. Come on! He lifted them with shaking hands. The money was underneath. Two wads of fives, one of tens, all in rubber bands. He swallowed, glancing over his shoulder. There must be a hundred quid in tens alone. Janis was right – she can't know how much she's got. Not unless she counts it every night, like a miser. And even if she does, she'll think she's made a mistake. I mean, one tenner out of this lot? One fiver?

Trembling, he peeled back the top tenner and jerked it free of its band. It tore slightly. He was more careful with the five, easing it out before cramming both notes in his pocket, Right. Careful now. No clues.

He forced himself to slow down and replace everything in the drawer exactly as he'd found it. He closed it, then backed slowly out of the room, checking the floor to see he hadn't dropped anything. He returned to his chair and sat shaking. He felt sick, and could scarcely believe what he'd just done. A part of him cried out that it was not too late – he could still put the money back and nobody would ever know. Except himself, of course. And at the same time a softer voice told him he might have taken more – much more, with only the same slim risk of detection.

The shaking had stopped by the time his grandmother returned, but he still felt sick, and didn't really enjoy the vanilla slice she'd brought for him to eat with his tea. He showed her Becky's card and they talked about his sister for a while, and then his grandmother got up and went to the bedroom. He grew cold when he heard her open a drawer, but she came back smiling with a five pound note in her hand.

'Here,' she said. 'Take this. Your mother tells me you've got a school trip next week, and I daresay a bit of extra pocket money will come in handy.'

He left soon after that. It was raining harder and he was glad, because it wet his face and nobody knew he was crying.

# FEROCIOUS BEAK

My fate, it seems, is ever to set out in hope and to return in black despair. This morning I was up betimes, eager to confront my destiny. I broke fast with Robinson, who expressed his intention to accompany me to the Museum, where I was to present my letter of introduction to Ottley, and thence to Leyland's studio at Queen Street with the letter I have for him. When I told him I preferred to go alone he demurred, saying he was responsible to my father for my well-being while in London. When I insisted he grew vexed, and in his anger seemed to express doubt as to whether, left to myself, I would present the letters at all; whereupon I upbraided him for an insolent fellow and stormed out.

Nothing here in London is as I had imagined it would be. Nothing. No sooner was I upon the street than I began to notice discrepancies between my mode of dress and the attire of those about me. Nor was I alone in noticing these, for I distinctly saw passers by nudge their companions and whisper at my approach, and it quickly became evident to me that I could scarcely have attracted greater attention had I gone besmocked like a yokel with a straw in my mouth.

I bowed my head and quickened my pace, feeling my cheeks burn; anxious only to fulfil my mission and be done with it. Perhaps, I thought, Robinson will help me acquire some modish attire in which to attend the Academy tomorrow.

I would have carried out my intention in the teeth of my discomfiture, had I not chanced at that moment to glimpse my strange, wild image in a window: my coat flapping about my puny frame as I stumped along, my hair a flaming mane no hat could hide; my nose the ferocious beak of some creature from the Pit. How could I present letters to these great men? I, a nit the foal of a louse, whom the very urchins laugh to behold? I thought of them: William Young Ottley, Keeper at the British Museum, whose permission I shall need to draw from the antique. Joseph Bentley Leyland, the eminent sculptor from Halifax who knows Chantry, Westmacott and Haydon; and the heart within me quailed.

84

I wandered, and found myself at last beside the river where I stood, gazing for a long time into dark waters. The sky too was dark before I forsook the Embankment and hired a man to drive me back to Paternoster Row, and the darkness of water and of sky came seeping into my soul as I pondered my forthcoming encounter with Robinson.

# THIS TIME NEXT WEEK

The rain cleared over Sunday night and Monday was a scorcher. Lunchtime, kids perched on the wall like birds on a wire or flopped on the field in shirtsleeves.

Tim lay on his back with an open copy of *Jane Eyre* over his face. He'd had a couple of restless nights and was nodding off, when Dilys plonked herself down beside him.

'Hi, Tim. You sleeping?'

'No, reading. I'm short-sighted.'

'Ha, ha, ha. Listen – I'm sorry about the other day.' Tim had avoided her since his encounter with her brother. 'Gerry likes to show off a bit in front of strangers but he doesn't mean anything by it, and he's all right, really.'

'Oh, aye.' He lifted the book an inch and looked at her. 'He's a regular prince, Dil. I can hardly wait to see him again.'

'Don't be like that, Tim. Hey – do you realise, this time next week we'll be on our way to Haworth?'

'Yeah.' He let the book cover his face again. He'd

thought of nothing else, night and day, since Saturday. He was beginning to wish he'd never heard of Haworth.

'Well, aren't you looking forward to it?'

'S'pose so. You?'

'Course.' She dug him in the ribs. 'Are you going to conduct your half of this entire conversation through that book, Tim South?'

'Why not?'

'I thought you might like to see this.'

'What is it?'

'Picture of the place we'll be staying at. You know – the hostel.'

'Let's have a look, then.' Tim sat up and Dilys handed him a postcard. It showed a large house with lawns and old trees around.

'Wow – it's a mansion, Dil. I always thought youth hostels were made out of old stables and stuff like that.' He turned the card over. 'Longlands, it's called. Must have belonged to some rich geezer. Here.' He gave it back to her. 'Where'd you get that?'

'Mrs Lindsay lent it to me. She sent for it, I guess.'

'Is she going with us?'

'Uh-hn. Mrs Linsday, Mr Barker and old Ellis.'

'Three of 'em.'

'Yes, and fifteen of us. Five each. I hope I'm in Mr Barker's group. He's nice. Looks a bit like Nick Kamen.'

'Huh! They've got two eyes apiece, that's about it.'

'Shut up!' She thumped him on the arm. 'Talking of lookalikes, have you unearthed anything about your mysterious ancestor yet?'

'Have I heck. There was nothing in the library, and I wouldn't know where else to look. He was probably just some bum, anyway.'

'Probably. I know one of his descendants is.'

86

They leapt to their feet and there was a short chase. Tim cornered Dilys at the back of the bike sheds, but the buzzer went before he could beat her to death with his copy of *Jane Eyre*.

# A PRETTY SMILE

I swear I had barely settled with the wretched cabman before Robinson descended on me, anxious to know how Leyland was and how I had fared at the Museum. I had steeled myself along the way and answered firmly that since I had not seen Leyland, I had no idea how he was, and that, not having been within a mile of the Museum, I had fared neither well nor ill there; whereupon he became extremely angry, cursing himself for not having insisted upon accompanying me, and demanding to know how I had spent my day.

I told him I had spent my day making myself as inconspicuous as possible, by reason of my outmoded apparel and frightful appearance. He replied that there was nothing amiss in my apparel and that my appearance, far from being frightful, was quite unremarkable. The smirks and titters I had encountered were products of my imagination, and if I meant to succeed here in London I had better learn to curb such fancies and look the world in the eye. His tirade closed with an ultimatum to the effect that, unless I presented my letters tomorrow as well as approaching the Academy itself, he would return to Leeds, leaving me to my own devices.

I might have defied him, saying that if it should come

to that I should no doubt manage splendidly, but I was aware that his return without me would cause my father great distress, and so I agreed to call upon Ottley and Leyland, and present myself at the Academy tomorrow.

At dinner I broached the subject of the Castle Tavern at Holborn, and of its illustrious landlord. I expressed my intention of going there this very evening to shake Tom Spring by the hand, and urged Robinson to accompany me. This he declined to do on the grounds that he had letters to write, and that besides he was not one for taverns or for prizefighters. He was barely civil, and saw fit to remind me that our financial resources are limited, and to advise an early night in view of tomorrow's commitment.

To hell with our financial resources, say I, and with tomorrow's commitment too, for I have this night shaken Tom Spring's hand, been vouchsafed the smile of a fair damsel, and have found besides a place in this city where good company is to be had, and where a man might feel at ease.

The Castle Tavern is an island of warm good fellowship in an ocean of cold indifference. It had no frontage on the street, and I was obliged to ask a fellow the way, which is through a carriage entrance into a courtyard. Sounds of merriment reached me the instant I entered this yard and, crossing it, I saw an open door and went in.

The room in which I found myself was warm, hazy with the smoke from many pipes and abuzz with animated conversation. It was curtained and upholstered in red, and on its walls were sporting prints, etchings and ornate chimney glasses in great profusion. At least forty men were in the room, seated in groups on chairs and benches at dark, lustrous tables on which stood great numbers of glasses and tankards.

I had barely entered when a fellow greeted me as though we had been acquainted all our lives, and I quickly found myself seated beside him among five others, each of whom shook me by the hand and urged me to act as arbiter in some argument they'd been having.

A fresh round of ale having been procured (and I having forborne to reveal my adherence to the Temperance Movement) my host told me the company had fallen to discussing famous battles, and disagreement had arisen as to the dates of some of these. 'I knew you for a man of education, sir,' he said, 'the instant I clapped eyes on you, and I said to my friends here, "Gentlemen, here's the fellow'll settle matters once and for all."' He winked at me over the rim of his tankard. 'You will umpire our little match, won't you, sir?'

I told him I felt flattered and would be delighted to arbitrate, though professing no great expertise in the field. Cries of good-natured disbelief greeted my disclaimer, as 'Oh no, not likely,' and, 'Come off it, Professor!' and then they commenced to mention a hodge-podge of battles both ancient and modern, some of them quite obscure. Nevertheless, I was able without difficulty to supply the dates they sought.

'Marathon,' says one.

'B.C. 490,' says I.

'There,' crows he to the company, 'what did I tell you?'

'The Armada,' says another.

'1588,' says I, and this is greeted with loud cheers. Men gather round to listen.

'Syracuse,' says a third.

'B.C. 413,' says I.

And after that, Chalons, Tours, Hastings, Blenheim and a number of others. Backs were slapped, noses tweaked, wagers settled. Throughout all of this a girl came and went, fetching and carrying. A veritable damsel, unless my indulgence after prolonged abstinence was causing me to see that which was not there. Once, this vision lingered a moment to hear what I was saying, and flashed me a smile before departing. A pretty smile, too. I see it still, and it disturbs me.

Presently, one of the company asked my name, and where I was from, and what my business might be in London. I told him my name was Alexander Percy, that I had left my father's estates in Ireland to study at the Royal Academy and that I was in fact a student there. With this, my stock seemed to rise even higher with them than it had stood before, and presently, when Mr. Tom Spring himself appeared, I was introduced to him under my assumed name.

The rest is hazy. We drank and laughed immoderately. I held my own. Nay, more than that. I found myself liked and respected: looked up to as a man of wisdom and of wit, and it was very late when we left the tavern and I allowed myself to be put into a cab. I think that we arranged to reassemble tomorrow evening and I shall certainly be there, if for no other reason than that I cannot forget that pretty smile and must see it again, or die.

# QUITE A PILE

The week dragged for the fifteen kids who'd signed up on the Haworth trip. The weather stayed fine, but on the Thursday came the first dark rumblings from the forecasters of a change at the weekend. Tim's mother got it from Michael Fish between the six o'clock news and 'Look North', and went to the foot of the stairs.

'Tim?' Tim was in his room, getting some of his stuff together. His mother's voice reawoke the worm of fear he'd carried in his guts since Saturday. He knew it was daft, but every time the phone rang or one of his parents called him he thought, this is it. They've found out. I've had it now. He went on to the landing.

'Yes, Mum?'

'You'd better pack your kagoul and overtrousers, love – they're talking about a change in the weather.'

He sighed his relief and called, 'Yes, Mum. I was anyway. They're on the list.'

Mrs Lindsay had given everybody a list. It included all the standard foul weather and emergency gear: strong boots, waterproofs, mint cake, a whistle. All of these things were in the bulging rucksack on his bedroom floor, together with a giant polybag, a torch, some matches in a tin, five pairs of thick woollen socks, a Swiss Army knife with a thing for getting jelly-babies out of pensioners' earholes and, in a small zip-pocket, two crumpled banknotes he preferred not to think about.

It was Sunday morning when the gunge hit the fan. The Souths had finished breakfast, and Michael Fish had been as good as his word because it was raining and blowing outside. Tim's dad, unable to wash the car, was doing the *Express* crossword in the front room while his wife washed up. Tim had retired to his room and was sitting on the bed, looking for the thousandth time at the picture of his mystery ancestor, when the phone rang.

Tim let the picture rest across his knees and sat absolutely still, listening. A Sunday morning phone call was unusual. Is this it? he wondered. The worm was wriggling in his stomach again, but there'd been so many false alarms that by now he didn't really believe he was going to be found out.

The telephone was in the hall. He heard his mother come from the kitchen and lift the receiver. He strained his ears. She was listening more than talking, and when she did say something Tim couldn't make out the words. After a minute the receiver pinged down and his mother went into the front room. A murmur of voices, footsteps, and his father at the foot of the stairs, calling 'Tim!'

Oh, God! This really is it. I can tell by the tone of his voice. Tim stood up, quaking. The picture slipped unnoticed to the floor and lay face down on the carpet. He crossed to the door, opened it and, fighting to keep his voice steady, called 'Yes, Dad?' What should he do? Admit it? Deny all knowledge? How did they know it was him? Had he left something – some damning evidence?

'Come down here, please.'

He crossed the landing and started down. Yes. This is it. No doubt whatever. Look at their eyes watching me. Grave expressions. Why did I do it? Why?

'What's up Dad, Mum?' Hang on. Find out what's what. How much they know.

'That was your grandma on the phone, Tim. She's

92

been burgled. Somebody's taken all her money. She sounds badly shaken, and your mum and I are going over there straight away. We'd like you to hang on here till we get back, okay?'

Tim gulped and nodded. 'Okay.' You bet it's okay, he thought. Better than okay in fact. His brain raced. All her money? All? Then somebody – somebody else must've—. He looked at his father. 'How much is missing?'

His father, helping his wife into her coat, shook his head. 'She doesn't know exactly. She kept quite a pile in the house, I think. A hundred, maybe two. It should've been in the bank, of course. Too late now.'

As the door closed behind his parents, Tim sank on to the bottom step and shook his head. Jeez, but that was close! Thank goodness I didn't say anything. Burgled! And I was about a thousandth of a millimetre away from the great confession. He laughed briefly. It's nothing to laugh at, mind. I mean, I ought to be feeling sorry. Poor old Grandma. All her savings.

But what a relief, though. What a let-off. It's all gone, and she's no idea how much was there. That means the burglar'll get the blame for all of it, including the fifteen quid I took. I'm off the hook. I don't even have to put it back, right? In fact I can't put it back, can I? Fifteen quid, suddenly appearing in that drawer? There's no way.

I wonder who did it?

# A Withered Leaf

Robinson is gone and I am alone in London. Here endeth a day of misery which began with an appalling scene near Somerset House.

We set out (nothing, this time, could dissuade Robinson from accompanying me) at nine thirty in the morning, armed with the letters to Ottley and Leyland, and another to Henry Howard, Secretary of the Royal Academy, with whom Robinson had got me an appointment for ten thirty. I was carrying examples of my work to show, since this is part of the procedure. My disposition was greatly improved from that of yesterday, and I felt that this time all would be well.

Imagine then my discomfiture when, immediately upon alighting from our conveyance outside Somerset House, I was suddenly smitten with the conviction that my work was not merely worthless, but laughable. Thus, on the very threshold of that portal beyond which lay my destiny I was undone, and the heart within me quailed. 'Robinson,' I said, 'I cannot.'

He tried sweet reason: I demurred. He harangued me: I was adamant. He waxed contemptuous: I wept.

Passers by lingered to satisfy their curiosity. The time of my appointment came, and passed. Finally, Robinson went off in a towering passion and left me to face the spectators alone, like a species of monkey with a folio under its arm.

Needless to say I presented no letters. Somerset House is adjacent to the river, and so once again I found myself beside its dark waters. I stood for hours, thinking about my father, and my Aunt, and all those others whose goodness has enabled me to undertake this venture, and I squirmed to think how poorly I repay their kindness; how utterly I fail to justify their faith in me.

I have longed to cut myself loose from my family; to stand alone and make them proud of me. Their condescension has oppressed me far too long, yet what am I apart from them:

> *A Withered leaf on Autumn's blast*
> *A shattered wreck on ocean's tide—.*

A monkey, laughed to scorn.

I gazed at the river, and its current soothed me like laudanum and carried away my pain, and I thought, 'What shadows we are, and what shadows we pursue.' At its source, the river is a crystal spring which bursts sparkling into sunlight and plunges, chattering brightly, down the hillside. Alas, though, its waters can travel only downwards. Once off the mountain, the way becomes first difficult, then tedious slow; until at last, fouled with its accumulation of mud and debris, it creeps sluglike to its journey's end and is swallowed by the sea. And our life's journey is the same; from the crystal spring of youth, downward, ever downward, to the black, boundless ocean of death.

Why then should I labour, since the end will be the same? Many paths lead to that ocean; some less tedious than others.

Who but a clod would choose tedium?

# FLIPPIN' BRIEF

Monday dawned cool and grey. Tim's mother handed him his packed lunch, pecked him on the cheek and told him to be careful, and his father drove him to school with his luggage. 'Don't give your teachers any trouble,' he warned, lifting the suitcase out of the boot. 'Remember you're in Haworth to learn, not to fool around. Enjoy yourself, and I'll see you on Friday.'

'Right.' Tim shouldered his rucksack and picked up the case. 'Thanks for the lift, Dad. See you.'

He was glad to get away. The break-in had left his grandmother in such a state that his parents had brought her back with them last night to stay for a few days. She'd been out when the burglary actually occurred – it was Saturday – but the thief had left no trace and she hadn't missed the money till Sunday morning. During his parents' absence, Tim had almost succeeded in convincing himself that the burglary had wiped his own slate clean. After all, if he hadn't taken the fifteen pounds the thief would have got it, wouldn't he? At least this way it was still in the family. But face to face, obliged to commiserate with the old lady, he'd felt his cheeks burn and hadn't been able to look her in the eye. He'd been relieved when she hadn't appeared at breakfast.

He carried his luggage to the changing rooms and dumped it with everybody else's. You can't book into a Youth Hostel before five in the afternoon, so the coach wasn't due to pick them up till half past ten. Even then, they'd have four or five hours to kill in Haworth before they could get into Longlands.

He was just leaving the changing rooms when Dilys staggered in. 'Oh hi, Dil. Here – let me take the case.' She relinquished it and Tim put it beside his own. 'Shove your rucksack here as well,' he said. 'We might get to sit together on the coach.'

Dilys dropped the rucksack, wiped her forehead with the back of a hand and looked at him. 'Who says I want to?'

Tim shrugged. 'Please yourself, only lasses usually fall over one another to sit next to me on coaches.'

'Oh, aye. Anyway, I thought you'd be sitting with Chris Barraclough and Alvin Cooper and that lot.'

'I might, seeing you're not bothered.'

'I never said I wasn't bothered. And anyway, it might be old Ellis who decides who sits with who. You know what he's like.'

Instead of going to their usual classes, the fifteen trippers assembled in a spare room for what was described as a final briefing. It began with a pep-talk from Ellis all about how, over the next few days, they were going to be representatives of Scorton Comprehensive – ambassadors, in fact. The people around them would judge the school by their appearance and conduct, and they should bear this in mind and behave accordingly. There was to be no shouting or running wild through the streets, no litter, no foul language and definitely no smoking. This trip was to be regarded not as a holiday, but as an extension of their work in school.

When Ellis had finished, Mrs Linsday produced a copy of her list and ran a verbal check to make sure everybody had brought the right stuff. You didn't have to have a picture of your great, great, great, great grandfather, but Tim had retrieved his from the floor and, without knowing why, had dropped it in his case on top of everything else.

After the baggage check Barker took over, droning on about Youth Hostels and how to behave in them. Lee Freeman leaned forward, tapped Tim on the shoulder and whispered, 'I thought briefings were meant to be flippin' brief.' He whispered a bit too loudly and Ellis heard him. Lee was sent out of the room, and Ellis filled in the fifteen minutes that remained with an impromptu harangue about manners.

Nobody was sorry when, at half past ten precisely, Lee popped his head round the door to announce that he'd just seen a mini-coach backing on to the drive.

# RACIST PIG

'Here, y'are, Dil!' Tim patted the vacant seat beside him and Dilys slipped into it. He grinned. 'You made it in the nick of time, kid – Trish and Cheryl were right behind you, jockeying for position. Spoilt their whole day, you have.'

'Oh sure. Ellis'll probably move us, anyway.'

She was right. As the teachers boarded, Ellis noticed that the Barraclough gang had bagged the long back seat. 'Oh, no, you don't.' He shook his head. 'I'm not having you four sitting back there where nobody can see you.' He studied the layout for a moment. 'Christopher Barraclough, change places with Dilys Williams. Lee Freeman – there's a seat at the front here beside Mr Barker, and Janis Clegg can come and sit with Mrs

Lindsay.' He waited till these manœuvres were completed, then moved up to the back and plonked himself down between Dilys and Alvin Cooper.

'Now then, Prof.' Chris smiled as he slid in beside Tim. 'Why didn't you come on the back seat – we saved a place for you?'

Tim shrugged. 'Wouldn't have made any difference, would it? You got split up.'

'Ah, but he might have left us if you'd been there. A nice, sensible guy to keep us in line and all that.'

'No chance. He's gone right off me since I told Dusty I was leaving. The whole staff has.'

'Knickers to 'em. Nine weeks next Monday, we're gone.'

The bus growled its way through Scorton to the M1. As it sped north, breaks appeared in the cloud, and by the time it turned on to the M62 an hour later the sun was out and the vehicle was racing its shadow westward.

At eleven forty-five they left the motorway and began passing through suburbs of Bradford, heading for Haworth. It was uphill most of the way. As the vehicle climbed, the suburbs thinned, giving way first to rolling meadow then bleak upland pasture, criss-crossed with ancient drystone walling. Hill farms, some of them derelict, squatted behind windbreaks of sycamore, rowan and oak, in a blasted landscape of reeds and heather, stones and sheep.

'Crikey!' breathed Dilys. 'No wonder *Jane Eyre*'s full of wind and storms and stuff. It'd do something to your brain, living in a place like this.'

Mr. Ellis beamed. 'That's right, Dilys. And the Brontës used weather and wild landscape to symbolise the moods and passions of their characters.' He smiled approvingly at the pupil whose remark had justified the expedition so early. Dilys had made his day.

It was just after twelve when the minicoach swung into the carpark at Haworth. As it rolled to a halt, Ellis got up and moved to the front. 'Right, folks, here we are.' He looked at his watch. 'It's five past twelve. The weather's fine, so what we'll do is leave everything on the bus and have a look round the village. There are toilets near the entrance to this carpark for those who need them, and there's an information centre at the top of the main street where you can pick up pamphlets, look at the maps and so forth. There's also the church, and plenty of interesting shops. Don't go into cafés – remember you've all got packed lunches and when you've had a look round, we'll eat. Don't go in the Parsonage Museum – we'll be doing that tomorrow. We're not going to shepherd you round like a crowd of infants, but remember – best behaviour, please. We'll meet back here at—.' He consulted his watch again. 'Twelve forty-five, precisely.'

They disembarked and walked through narrow streets. Chris put on a spurt to catch up with Lee, and Tim slowed down to wait for Dilys, who was walking with Cheryl. 'Well,' he said, 'this is it, girls. Brontëland.' He inhaled deeply. 'Smell that inspiration.'

'That's fresh air, you div,' said Dilys. 'It wouldn't have smelled like this in their day. Ellis reckons it ponged a bit.'

'Yes.' Cheryl's eyes shone with relish. 'Dung-heaps by all the cottages, factory chimneys belching smoke and an open sewer running right down the middle of here.'

They were at the top of the steep, cobbled main street. It was thronged with sightseers who wandered up and down, or gathered in little crowds in front of shop windows. There were pushchairs, cameras, dogs.

'Look at that,' said Tim. 'I thought Haworth was a quiet little village in the hills, and it turns out to be a shopping centre, swarming with Japanese.'

Alvin hurried by, looking for the rest of the gang. 'Velly big in Tokyo,' he laughed. 'The Blontës.'

'Racist pig!' cried Dilys, as he went off down the slope.

## PRETTY BIG

It was twenty past five when they got to the hostel. They'd all seen it on the postcard but it looked different close up. Dark, massive and somehow forbidding. A Victorian mansion built to impress; built to last.

'Pretty big, huh?' murmured Dilys, gazing at the great square porch. Tim nodded. It made him feel creepy just looking at it.

Inside it felt different. It was warm. There was a little shop with drinks and sweets and stuff, and soft chairs round a coffee table. There was a staircase like something out of a movie, with a great stained-glass window on the half-landing. And there was a woman called Dawn who smiled and talked to them while old Ellis saw to the paperwork with her husband.

The house was on three floors. 'You'll be sleeping in the attics,' said Dawn. 'We're expecting a party of younger children tomorrow and we're putting them on the first floor. Pick up your luggage and I'll show you where you are.'

There were two attic dormitories. One was big, the other small. Both were equipped with a number of double bunks. There were sloping ceilings with beams, and windows with views of the grounds. The six girls got the small room and the boys got the big one because there were nine of them. They dumped their things, and Dawn showed them the washrooms, the TV lounge and the shelf at the top of the cellar steps for muddy boots. They found out where the dining room was, and learned that the Warden's kitchen was out of bounds. There were groans when Dawn revealed that the teachers would be sleeping in the rooms with them, and cheers when she showed them the games room in the cellar with a pool table and Space Invaders machine.

At half past six, when they'd unpacked and settled in, there were sausages and chips for dinner. They went from the dining room to the schoolroom, where a Countryside Warden gave them a talk about the area. He showed slides, and told them how sometimes, in the hills, the weather can change drastically in a matter of minutes. He said it was not unknown for somebody to set off for a walk in light clothing on a warm spring day, get caught by a change in the weather, and be dead before anyone could reach them. 'Always carry warm, windproof gear with you,' was his message.

Chris reckoned the man was talking rubbish, and said so to those around him. 'This is England,' he whispered, 'not the flippin' Arctic. How can you be sweltering one minute and freezing to death the next? He's just trying to scare us 'cause we don't live round here.'

When the talk was over, they were free to do more or less as they pleased till bedtime. Some people went down to the games room. Others explored the grounds, or the house itself. Tim felt like being alone so he went up to the dorm. He'd bought a postcard from the shop downstairs. It was a picture of the stained-glass window. He turned it over, addressed it to his parents and wrote:

'Trip's okay
Chips okay
Kip's okay –
    Tim.'

He'd post it in the village tomorrow.

## NOTHING DAUNTED

Upon my return to Paternoster Row I was handed a note. It was from Robinson, and informed me that he had vacated the Coffee House and was returning to Leeds. He had deposited some money for my use with the proprietor; sufficient, he reckoned, for three to four days and my journey home. The note went on to express his disappointment at my conduct (it could scarcely have been more bitter than my own) and closed with his fervent hope that I might yet summon the strength to accomplish my purpose.

'Hang your disappointment, Robinson!' I cried, as I crumpled his note and hurled it into a corner, 'and likewise your fervent hope.'

I recalled that I was expected that evening at the Castle Tavern, and the memory of the smile I had been vouchsafed there rendered my attendance imperative. I changed, dined and, having relieved the proprietor of my funds, arrived at Holborn shortly after nine o'clock.

I was greeted by the admirable Spring, who demonstrated the excellence of his memory by addressing me as Percy, but of my companions of last evening there was no sign. Nothing daunted, I carried my glass to a corner from which I might observe the comings and goings of the damsel.

Presently, my glass being empty I summoned her, and was gratified when she flashed me the twin of last evening's smile. I asked her name.

'My name, sir?' Dark eyes twinkling under arched brows. 'My name is Clare Connor. Why d'you ask?'

I made no answer, but asked, 'Why did you smile at me yesterday, Clare Connor?' The drink had made me bold.

'You are a customer, sir,' she replied. ''Tis my duty to make you feel welcome.'

'Yet you do not smile at all of the patrons,' I said. 'I have watched you, and I know.'

She blushed, becomingly. 'If you want the truth, sir, 'tis this: I am Irish, and had heard that you are also from across the water.'

'You hear aright,' I told her. 'I am Alexander Percy. My father's estates are in Ireland, though I am presently a student at the Royal Academy.'

'Yes, sir. I have heard that also.' She held up the glass. 'What's your pleasure, sir – brandy?'

I smiled and said, 'My pleasure, fair maid, is your company. I trust it is not your intention to divest me of it so soon?'

'Twas Percy who spoke so: I would never have dared. She blushed more deeply. 'Sir,' she protested, 'I have my duty to attend to. These other gentlemen—.'

'Gentlemen?' I glanced about with Percy's cool disdain. 'I see no gentlemen. Stay.'

She would not, but fetched my brandy and went about her business, followed hither and thither by my eyes until my emptying glass obliged her to attend me again. As the spirit loosened my tongue I began to press her: had she free time tomorrow? Might I see her, away from the inn? She replied, laughing that she had not; that I might not. 'You will see me here, sir,' she said at last, 'in the evening, if you come.'

'Oh, I shall come,' I vowed, gazing into a glass which, though nearly empty, was not as empty as my purse. 'Neither Scylla nor Charybdis shall keep me from thy side.'

I did not say it. Percy did. Percy, and the drink.


# TIMMO HAUNTED

The bunks were a novelty and nobody slept much that first night, but it wasn't nearly as much fun as it might have been. They could have talked and swapped jokes and played scary tricks on one another, but with the teachers there it was a non-starter.

Mrs Lindsay read the girls some Brontë poems and a bit out of *Jane Eyre*. The boys talked and messed about a bit, but old Ellis killed the lights at half past ten and that was that. At midnight, Christopher Barraclough had to go to the washroom and just happened to bump into Janis Clegg, but that was their secret.

Everybody was up by seven thirty. They washed, dressed, made their beds and went down to breakfast. After breakfast they spent twenty minutes tidying the dorms and collecting their packed lunches before the coach came to take them up to the village.

The Parsonage didn't open till eleven, so they went into the dim, grave-crammed churchyard and strolled among the stones, reading epitaphs. It was chilly. The long grass was drenched with dew and nesting rooks clamoured in the trees.

Tim leaned against a tree trunk with his hands in his pockets, looking at his boots. He didn't like graveyards. He never had. He couldn't understand what people got out of reading gravestones and looking at the flowers people left. Cemetery flowers are love gifts to dead people, but the dead have gone where even love can't reach. They don't smell flowers.

'Hey, Prof – what's up?'

'Huh?' Tim looked up and saw Lee grinning at him across the weathered slabs. 'Oh, nothing. I don't like graveyards, that's all.'

'Scared of ghosts, are you?'

Tim smiled wanly. 'Something like that.' It wasn't that, of course. It was just graveyards, and this one in particular, but he didn't feel like talking to Lee about it.

'Some of the kids have gone inside the church with Mr Barker,' said Lee. 'You coming?'

'Sure. Why not?'

He felt a bit better in the church. There was a smell in churches which he liked. He didn't know what caused it – candles perhaps, or age, or holiness. When he was small he'd assumed it was holiness. You breathed it in and it made you feel better, which was what you'd expect. Anyway, he liked it.

After the church, Tim tagged along with a group which was going to the Sunday School. Mr Barker told them Branwell Brontë taught there before he became a drunkard and a drug addict, but when they got to it, it was closed. 'Never mind,' said the teacher. 'I've mentioned Branwell's vices, so we might as well see the shop where he got his dope and the pub where he did his boozing.'

By the time they'd done these things, and visited the information centre, the sun had taken the chill off the morning and the Parsonage was open. Old Ellis gathered everybody together.

'Right, folks. In a few minutes we'll be going into the Parsonage Museum, which is probably the most important place we'll see on this trip. It's where the Brontës were actually living when they wrote their novels. It is where Charlotte wrote *Jane Eyre*, and I want you to think about that as we walk round. I expect you to conduct yourselves in a civilised fashion, remembering that the Parsonage is not only a museum, but a shrine. People come here like pilgrims from all over the world, and I'd like you to think about that, too.'

They trooped into the Parsonage garden. 'Stand by to be bored out of your skull,' muttered Alvin to nobody in particular. Mr Ellis bought eighteen tickets at the door and they were in.

There were four rooms downstairs, done out to look like they did in the Brontës' day. You couldn't go in them. You looked from behind a rope. There were old carpets, chairs and pictures, and tables with objects on them – books and quill pens and stuff. There was a long clay pipe, a top hat and a magnifying glass in one room, and an old copy of *Jane Eyre* in another. There wasn't a lot of space, and the kids who were interested jostled one another to get to the front. Others lingered in the

107

corridor looking fed up. Alvin was one of these. 'Told you, didn't I?' he grumbled. 'Boring. You could look in a junkshop window and see the same stuff for nowt.'

The three teachers dodged about, trying to make sure kids didn't set off any alarms or get in other visitors' way. Ellis bobbed up and down in the kitchen doorway, trying to see over people's heads. 'Come on, folks. Move on when you've had a look. People are waiting.'

Tim stood motionless on the threshold of Mr Brontë's study. He seemed to be gazing at the objects in the room, but he was not. It was a hundred and fifty years from now, and he was in his parents' house, a shrine visited by the countless fans of Timothy South, O.B.E. (1975–2076), author, wit and genius, whose sparkling career had spanned two centuries. The house was crammed with adoring pilgrims, and the queue outside stretched three quarters of the way down Anemone Way. The most popular room in the house was Tim's Room. A card on the wall told visitors that this was the very room in which the genius played and slept as a child. In it were his bed, his ancient Sony Walkman, a rocking horse called Silver and a framed photograph of his tragic sister, shot dead while robbing a bank in 1993.

'South!'

Tim jumped and turned. Old Ellis was glaring down at him over the heads of a knot of tourists. 'S-sir?'

'Wake up lad, for goodness sake. The others are all upstairs.'

Upstairs were more rooms, all roped off. Tim peered into a couple, then tagged on the end of a long queue, shuffling past some glass cases. He quite liked *Jane Eyre*, and he supposed it was marvellous to think he was actually in the house where it was written, but he was getting a bit cheesed off just the same. It was a nice enough museum, but when you've seen one roped-off room you've seen 'em all, and something about the place depressed him.

He was peering through glass at a tiny handwritten book, trying to make out some of the words, when he heard Chris Barraclough's voice. 'Hey look – there's a picture of old Timmo here!' Some of the kids laughed and Chris called out 'Hey, Prof – come here a minute. I didn't know you were a Brontë-flippin'-saurus!'

Tim flushed. What was the prannock on about? Visitors were looking about angrily, trying to see who was making all the noise. Chris called out again, and Tim began pushing through the crowd, anxious to shut him up. He spotted Mr Barker with a face like thunder, heading the same way.

Tim got there first. Chris and some of the others were gathered round a large white card with a picture on it. It was a man's head, done in cartoon style, and it did look quite like him. But what caught Tim's eye and caused his heart to kick was a smaller picture in a glass case beside it. It was a framed silhouette in profile, identical to the one he'd found at home.

# I HAVE MY CLARE

Fragile from too much brandy, I spent the greater part of the day in my bed. Like the estimable Percy I am become nocturnal in my habits: a creature of the night. I lay, watching the play of light and shadow in my room as the sun crossed the heavens. Hail to the sun, whose unflattering rays light up our imperfections, exposing us to ridicule and scorn. Hail, and farewell.

At twilight I left my room and flew with joy to Holborn and to Clare. She smiled. I drank. We conversed. Passion smouldered in me. As the evening passed I grew more bold, she more complaisant, until, by a subterfuge whose particulars now elude me, we contrived to be together in her room at the top of the house. There she gave herself to me, and there I left my likeness for a keepsake.

So that now, dogged though my footsteps have been by cruel misfortune, and dogged though they may be in the time to come, there is this: that one who left his home a callow youth will return as a man.

Nelson had his Emma, Bonaparte his Josephine. Great men, great loves. And I? I have my Clare.

# A Matching Pair

Tim gazed at the silhouette. 'Who is it?' he murmured.

Chris laughed. 'It's you, you lossock. Who else is there with a conk like that?'

The laughter died as Mr Barker arrived on the scene. 'What's going on here, Barraclough – I can hear you shouting in the next room.'

'It's this picture, sir. It looks like South.'

The teacher barely glanced at the portrait. 'You mean to tell me the sole reason for all this fuss is an imagined resemblance between this portrait and South? How old are you, lad?'

'Nearly sixteen, sir.'

'Quite. And if I didn't know that, Barraclough – if I was one of these visitors whose peace you've disturbed – I'd guess from your behaviour that you were eight, or possibly nine. It's juvenile, lad. What is it?'

'Juvenile, sir.'

'Right. I think you'd better stay with me till we get outside.' He glared at the others. 'The rest of you can move on, but don't let me hear any more noise.'

The group dispersed, looking sheepish. Tim lingered long enough to read what was on the card, then wandered out of the room and downstairs into the crowded souvenir shop, his thoughts in a whirl.

Branwell Brontë. The picture was of Branwell Brontë, and it was the same as the one in his suitcase back at the hostel.

No. He shook his head. It can't be. It's too fantastic. I've made a mistake. Sure, the two guys are similar. Glasses and big noses, but there's lots of guys like that. There's me, for a kickoff. If the chap in my picture was Branwell Brontë, it'd mean—.

Tim glanced about him. Most of the kids were in the shop now. Barker was there with Chris in tow, and Mrs Lindsay was at the far end looking at a book. Old Ellis didn't seem to have come down yet, but the place was packed and it was hard to tell.

Tim wasn't feeling too good. There was a sort of excitement deep down which he was struggling to suppress, and the effort was making him feel sick. It was hot in the shop and everybody seemed to be looking at him. He was standing in front of a fixture full of picture postcards. He wasn't really looking at them – his mind was too messed up for that – but his eyes slid across them and stopped at one with Branwell on it. It was

111

like the picture upstairs, only smaller. It was like——.

He plucked it from the rack and went and stood in line to pay. He turned it over. Patrick Branwell Brontë, he read. The only known portrait.

When he'd paid he left the shop and flopped down on a bench. He was shaking. He looked at the postcard. It was like the picture he'd found in the attic. He was almost sure now that he had a matching pair. He shivered.

The shop door opened. Dilys and Cheryl came out clutching small paper bags. Tim turned the postcard face down on his lap and covered it with his palm. The girls joined him on the bench.

Cheryl fanned herself. 'Phew! It's like an oven in there. What d'you get, Tim?'

'Nothing.'

'Yes, you did! I was behind you in the queue. Let's have a look.'

'No.'

'Oh, go on – I'll show you mine, look.' She opened her bag and tipped out two cards and a pencil. 'Now yours.'

'No.'

'Miserable pig. Isn't he miserable, Dil?'

Dilys leaned forward and looked at Tim. 'Why won't you show us what you bought, Tim – something disgusting, is it? A bit of porn, like? You've a funny look on your face.'

'Don't talk daft.'

'Well, then?'

'It's a card. Just a card with Branwell's picture, like the one upstairs.'

'What – the one Chris was yelling about? What d'you want that for – d'you think it really looks like you?'

'No.'

'Why, then?'

He shrugged, reluctant to speak in front of Cheryl. 'Dunno. Might write home on it.'

'You wrote home already,' said Cheryl. 'I saw you post it first thing.'

'My gran. I might send to my gran.'

'Hmm! Anybody'd think we were here for a month.'

'It's nothing to do with you who I write to.'

'Never said it was, did I? Come on, Dil.'

They got up and moved away. Tim gazed after them. He'd have liked to talk to Dilys, but not with Cheryl there. Dil would've listened and told him what she thought. Cheryl would have laughed her head off.

He looked round. Kids were coming out of the shop. In a few minutes the teachers would appear, and then they'd be off with their packed lunches to some place called the Brontë Waterfall. All he wanted to do was rush back to Longlands and see the two pictures side by side. He looked at his watch. Jeez, was that all? Quarter past twelve? It felt like three o'clock already.

Doesn't time fly when you're having fun?

# IN THE MIDDLE OF MAY

It was heavy going. The sun shone, they were all kitted out with boots and rucksacks, and it was uphill a lot of the way. Tim loitered, wanting to be last so he could think, but Chris and Alvin hung back too, and by the time they left the road to strike out over the moor Lee and Janis had joined them.

'Blow this for a game of soldiers,' grumbled Chris. He was breathing hard and his forehead glistened with sweat. 'I don't see why we have to lug all this gear in the middle of May.' They were wearing t-shirts and other light stuff, but in their rucksacks were kagouls and overtrousers, thick woollen socks and other foul weather equipment.

Tim shrugged. 'You know what the guy said last night. It can change in minutes.'

'Can it, heck!' Chris indicated the sky with a sweep of his hand. 'Look. No clouds. You don't get rain without clouds, dickhead.'

Tim didn't reply. He was thinking about the postcard in his back pocket and couldn't be bothered arguing. The other three agreed with Chris, and a discussion started about how they might lighten their loads for tomorrow's long hike.

They reached the waterfall just before one o'clock. It came down the side of a narrow valley and into a stream. A stone bridge spanned the stream. Old Ellis told them it was known as the Brontë Bridge. Janis grinned and whispered that if there was a rubbish tip nearby it would probably be known as the Brontë rubbish tip.

They sat on boulders to eat lunch. Mrs Lindsay read out a poem by Emily Brontë, and Mr Barker explained how Charlotte used stone and water as symbols in *Jane Eyre*. 'They should've brought the flippin' exam paper,' whispered Lee. 'We could've done it and got it over with.'

After lunch some of the kids went off up the valley. Others removed their boots and paddled in the icy

114

stream. Tim stretched out on the springy turf with his rucksack under his head, closed his eyes and let his thoughts drift.

Branwell Brontë. A drunkard, Barker had called him. A drug addict. A drunkie-junkie who wrote stories as a kid and died young. That was all Tim knew about him, but there had to be more to his life than that. Are there any books about him, and why the heck do I care, just because I'm supposed to be some kind of look-alike? He shook his head to drive away the phantom.

The lumpy feel of the rucksack made him remember his grandma's fifteen pounds. It was still there in the zip pocket. He hadn't even looked at it. He didn't know whether he'd be able to touch it when the time came. He wished he'd left it for the burglar. He wished he could think about *Jane Eyre* like he was supposed to, instead of worrying over a stupid picture and a few quid the thief would have taken if *he* hadn't.

Walking back, they were supposed to try to experience the environment with all of their senses. Bleak, harsh solitude. Hiss of wind through heather. Boggy reek of peat. Resilient turf and bruising millstone grit. 'Imagine you are poets,' said Mrs Lindsay. 'What sorts of stimuli would move you in this land? what symbols would you find – what metaphors?'

'Symbols,' growled Alvin. 'Metaphors. It's flippin' hot, there's cow-all to look at and I'm busting for a pee – how's that?'

When they got back to the hostel, the little kids had arrived. There were thirty of them and they seemed to be everywhere. There were two in the girls' attic till Mrs Lindsay's yell sent them squealing downstairs.

Tim didn't feel like dinner. When everybody had

gone down, he knelt and pulled his suitcase out from under the bed. He took out the portrait, placed it on the floor and put the postcard down beside it. He looked from one to the other and back again and swallowed hard.

'Snap!' he murmured.

# THE COLD LIGHT OF DAY

How true is that commonplace which states that things look different in the cold light of day! The vision I had of this city was a thousand times more grand than anything my eyes have beheld since I have been here. And the same is probably true regarding our pre-conceptions of less tangible aspirations: a studentship at the Royal Academy for example, or a place at the tables of the famous. Viewed from afar, these things seem as fabulous destinies sought by many and attained by a few, whose felicity thereafter is scarcely to be imagined. And yet I suspect that having scaled the heights, few find the view worth the climb. A man might as well follow the plough, since all roads lead to death, and the grave is a leveller.

And so to Clare. Viewed as they were late at night, and from the sort of distance fine brandy will interpose, the events of last evening filled me with exultation, so that my life seemed transformed. I was Napoleon. I was Horatio. I was Percy. Exalted by the greatest love the world has known, there seemed nothing to which I might not aspire.

And yet, viewed in the cold light of day, what is it? A personable young gentleman with silver on his tongue and gold in his pocket seduces a simple wench. It is a romp; a roll in the hay; another conquest in Percy's life of conquests. Oh, I daresay words were spoken; vows exchanged in the heat of the moment. But in the cold light of day she's a tavern wench and I'm a gentleman. Further dalliance could only cause her pain and besides, word might reach my father.

Percy would laugh and go his careless way. Why then should I feel shame?

## RUINOUS CHILD

'Dil?'

It was eight o'clock. Most of the kids were either down in the games room or watching TV. Dilys was sitting on her bunk writing a postcard when Tim stuck his head round the door.

'What d'you want, Tim?'

'I want to show you something.'

'What?'

'A picture. Two, actually.'

'You wouldn't show me and Cheryl this morning.'

'I was worried, Dil. Scared. Come here a minute and I'll show you why.'

Dilys sighed and stood up. 'This had better be good, Tim South. I was writing home and if I don't get it posted tomorrow I'll be there before it.'

They went to the boys' dorm. Tim said, 'Remember

that picture I told you about – the one I found in our attic?'

Dilys nodded. 'You told me about it but I've never seen it.'

'Well, this is it.' He handed her the portrait. 'Does it remind you of anyone?' She walked over to a window, tilted the card to catch the light and looked at it, frowning. 'It's familiar in a way,' she said. 'If it was dressed modern it could be you.'

Tim shook his head. 'I don't mean that, Dil. I mean, have you seen a picture like it recently – this morning, for instance?'

Dilys studied the silhouette again and shrugged. 'Don't think so. Why?'

'Look at this.' He gave her the postcard.

Dilys studied the portraits for a moment, then flipped the postcard over and read the back. She looked at Tim. 'You're winding me up, aren't you? This isn't the picture you told me about. You've copied this yourself from the postcard.'

'I haven't Dil, honestly. Look at that card. It's ancient. And anyway, where the heck would I get pens and indian ink?'

Dilys didn't reply. She compared the pictures again, carefully. She brushed a finger across the old card to feel how the ink stood up off the discoloured surface. She turned it over and looked at the marks on the back. Then she said, 'They're practically the same, Tim, but this is Branwell Brontë, and Branwell never married, did he? If he died a bachelor, he can't be this ancestor of yours, can he?'

Tim shrugged. 'Why not? You don't have to be married to have a baby.'

'I know, but—.' She gave him back the portraits and

118

shook her head. 'It's too fantastic, Tim. It's like one of your tall stories. I mean, think what a sensation it'd cause if it were true. Everybody thinking the Brontës died out a hundred years ago, and then this kid from Scorton turns up and says, "Hi, folks – I'm Branwell's – what was it?"'

'Great, great, great, great grandson.'

Dilys shook her head again. 'That's too many greats, Tim. Who'd remember after all this time? Who could prove anything?' She giggled. 'You'd own the museum, d'you realise that?' A thought struck her. 'Hey – do your folks come from around here?'

'Not that I know of.'

'Well, there you are, then. How could Branwell Brontë possibly be your ancestor if your folks come from somewhere else?'

'London.' Tim held up the old card. 'My gran says this guy ruined her great, great grandmother in London.'

'So how could old Branwell ruin somebody in London? There was no M1 you know.'

'No, but people did go to London, didn't they? There were coaches and trains.'

Dilys nodded. 'Right. So what you need to know is, was Branwell ever in London. D'you know what year this ruinous child happened, by any chance?'

'Sure. 1835. It's on the back of the card.'

'Well – find out if Branwell went to London and if so when, and if the dates match up, bingo! You'll have to stand very still in a glass case up at the museum for the rest of your life.'

Tim smiled wryly. 'It's not funny, Dil. It's scary. How can I find out about Branwell, anyway?'

'Ask old Ellis.'

'You're joking! I'm not telling him all this.'

'You don't have to, dummy. Just say you're interested in Branwell, and you'd like to know more about him. He's got books and stuff – I bet he'll be dead chuffed to lend you one.'

'Okay, I will. D'you happen to know where I can find him?'

'I know where he was a while back. He was down in the lobby, reading.'

'Thanks, Dil. For not laughing, I mean. Most people would.'

Dilys smiled and went back to her postcard. Tim found Mr. Ellis in the lobby and told him of his interest in Branwell Brontë. As Dilys had predicted, the teacher was delighted. 'I have Gerin's biography of Branwell in my bag,' he said. 'Follow me and I'll get it for you.'

Halfway down the backstairs at Longlands there's a ledge that's handy for sitting on. It's directly above the hot water tank so it's quite warm, even in the middle of the night. Tim found this ledge at nine o'clock, and he was still there at two in the morning.

Books are funny things. Now and then you'll pick up a book you can't put down. And sometimes, just occasionally, someone finds a book and reads it, and it changes his whole life.

## A MAN BEGUILED

It is finished, and the wench is to blame.

I took leave of my senses to pursue her; I was a man

120

beguiled. Now I must abandon my dream and flee; I am a man betrayed.

Not one hour ago a well-wisher, a patron of the Castle named Woolven came to me at the Chapter to inform me of certain events at the tavern, and to advise my early departure. How he knew where to find me I know not, but it is well for me that he did.

It seems that in my cups I had made some sort of promise to return to Clare last evening. When I did not, she became first agitated, then distraught. Noticing her condition, Spring questioned her and the wench told all. It transpires she is an orphan, and his ward. I swear that had I known this, I would have resisted her charm out of the profound respect I feel for the fellow. As it is he seeks me, not sorrowing, but wrathfully, and with the help of many friends.

I enjoy this single advantage: that they seek a man named Percy, a student of the Academy School. On the other hand they have my likeness, and so I find myself rattling northward, not gaily after the manner of Percy but apprehensively and with my hat pulled down, after the manner of myself.

Nothing is as it ought to be. Nothing. I have sought splendour and found squalor, independence and found inadequacy, conquest and am defeated.

Oh, that we might unmake the world and mould it closer to our hearts' desire!

# THINK

Can't sleep. Can't stop thinking about him. What's the time, for Pete's sake? Tim extricated his left arm from the sleeping bag. These bunks squeak like mad and Tariq's up above. He squinted at his watch. 02.44. Quarter to flippin' three. He sighed and closed his eyes. The light from his watch had left a floating green blob. He watched it till it began to fade, then opened his eyes. They burned from too much reading.

Branwell Brontë was in London in 1835.

He screwed up his aching eyes. This is stupid. I'm going to be shattered on that nine mile walk.

It fits though, doesn't it? Not just the trip to London and the year. Everything. He was short. He had red hair and specs. He dreamed up a whole fantasy world as a kid – Angria, he called it. He even shared it with his sister.

And what about when he grew up? Well, he never did, really, did he? I mean, he kept expecting the real world to be like his fantasy world, and when it wasn't he didn't want to know. He wanted to be like one of his heroes but there was no way because he was just this quiet, ugly little guy that people laughed at.

And who does all this remind you of, folks? Come on – think. Who do you know who's small and ugly with ginger hair and glasses, who doesn't like the way he looks or the way things are, so he goes round dreaming up stories with himself as the hero?

All right – I'll give you a clue. His latest thing is boozing and doing dope on an old barge. Oh, and pinching money. I nearly forgot that bit.

Have you got it now?

# THE DEMON DRINK

'And what did you make of old Branwell, South?' Ellis fussed about his immaculate bed, straightening, smoothing, tucking. Breakfast was in five minutes.

'He – had a rotten life, sir.'

Ellis nodded. 'Tragic, South.' He lifted his jacket from the back of a chair and shrugged it on. 'Clever lad, but unstable. Never could stick at anything. Terrible waste.'

'He was a bit of a dreamer, sir, wasn't he?'

'Oh, yes. Fantastic imagination, and of course there's nothing wrong with that. As the old song says:

> *You've got to have a dream*
> *If you don't have a dream*
> *How you gonna have a dream come true?*

'You heard that one, South?'

'I think so, sir.'

'The human imagination's a powerhouse, lad. All progress has been due to it – all our art, our philosophy, our technology. Imagination, harnessed by intellect. Branwell's trouble was that he blunted his intellect with the demon drink. He couldn't control his dreams. They took over, till in the end he couldn't distinguish between truth and fiction.'

'No, sir.'

Ellis bent and pulled a holdall from under the bed. He opened it, dropped the biography in and shoved it out of sight. 'We can dream of a better world, South, and we can work to make it come true, but some things can't be changed and we've just got to put up with them as they are. Coming to breakfast?'

# BEGINS BESIDE THE CHURCHYARD HERE

The coach dropped them in the village at nine twenty, kitted out for walking. It was chilly but the sky was clear. They mustered on the car park and Ellis spoke to them.

'The walk we're doing today is called the Brontë Way,' he began.

'Surprise, surprise,' muttered Chris. Tim grinned because he knew his friend expected it but he didn't feel like grinning. He was dog-tired and not looking forward to the day.

'It begins beside the churchyard here, and takes us nine miles to Wycoller in Lancashire. There are a number of interesting things to look out for in Wycoller, and I'll be mentioning some of them when we get there. The main attraction as far as we're concerned is Wycoller Hall, the house on which Charlotte Brontë based Ferndean Manor in *Jane Eyre*. It's a ruin, but it'll be interesting just the same.'

'Oh, aye.' Chris nodded. 'I can hardly wait.'

Ellis looked at him. 'Did you say something, Barraclough?'

'Yessir. I said I can hardly wait, sir.'

'Splendid.' If Ellis suspected that Chris was winding

him up he didn't show it. He went on to talk about the sort of terrain they'd be walking over, while Janis Clegg turned to Chris.

'Nine miles,' she groaned. 'Just to look at a flippin' ruin. Why can't we go on the coach?'

Chris grinned. 'You can't soak up the authentic Brontë atmosphere from a coach, you div. And anyway, you won't be doing nine miles.'

'How d'you mean?'

'Follow me.'

Chris began a slow drift towards the rear of the group. Janis followed. Touching Tim's shoulder, Chris hissed, 'Back here, Branwell.'

Tim looked round. 'Don't call me that.'

'Why not – you look just like him.'

'Because I don't like it, that's why.'

'Okay, okay – sssh!' Chris pressed a finger to his lips. 'Come over here.'

Hidden from the teachers by the other kids, Chris whispered, 'Listen. Me and Lee and Alvin aren't going on this jaunt. We don't fancy it. We've made plans. Look.' He slid the rucksack off his shoulder, plonked it on the ground and unbuckled the flap to reveal a double row of ringpull cans. 'Ale,' he grinned. 'Twelve cans. Weighs a flippin' ton. Lee's got another dozen, and Alvin's carrying fags and grub and all like that. We're gonna slope off and have a nice easy day.'

'How?' demanded Janis. 'With one teacher up front, another in the middle and one behind. That's how they go, you know.'

'I know. It's all taken care of.'

'How you gonna do it?'

'We. How are *we* going to do it – you're both invited. What we do is, we get ahead. I've already told Ellis I

125

can't wait, right? So we go like the clappers till we've left everybody well behind, then sneak off and lie low till they pass.'

Janis shook her head. 'It won't work. They'll call us back – make us stay with the group.'

'No, they won't. It's not like if we were planning to loiter behind. They wouldn't fall for that, but this way they'll just think we're keen. They'll be able to see us till the very last minute, and when we've sloped off they'll think we're just round the next bend or something. They won't know we've gone till they hit this Wycoller dump, and by then it'll be too late.'

'I don't think I'm going to do it,' said Tim.

Chris frowned. 'Why not? Just because I called you Branwell?'

'No.'

'What, then? Scared of the trouble after, are you?'

'No. I just want to go to Wycoller, okay?'

'You're a wally, aren't you, Bran? Deep down I mean. A right wally. You'd better not say owt to the teachers then. If we come unstuck we'll know who split.'

'I wouldn't split, Chris. I'm not joining you, that's all.'

Tramping up the side of the churchyard they heard excited yells and saw some of the little kids from the hostel. They were chasing one another round the gravestones under the watchful eye of a young woman who guarded their coats and knapsacks. Ellis passed her and the two exchanged sympathetic grins, as teachers do when they encounter one another on excursions. Tim, watching the kids, saw in the dimness under the trees another teacher, a man, standing motionless in the shadow of the far boundary wall. His eyes slid past and then something – something about the figure's stance or mode of dress made him backtrack, and when he did so the man was gone. He shook his head, knuckled his aching eyes and told himself it was a trick of the light.

He was trying to remember where he'd encountered a similar phenomenon when he felt a tug on his sleeve and Dilys said, 'How'd you get on last night, Tim – did you find anything out?'

'Yes, Dil, I did, and I don't know whether I'm glad or not. Listen.' Briefly, he outlined the story of Branwell Brontë's life as told in the book he'd read last night. He told her of the man's 'downcast smallness', his dissatisfaction with the real world and the fantasy world he created to replace it. He told her of Branwell's journey to London and of the mystery surrounding his activities there. His ignominious return, and his refusal to talk about the matter. By the time he'd finished, Haworth was behind them and they were striding the bleak tops.

'It's fantastic, Tim,' she murmured. 'The way it all fits. He's so like you.' She smiled briefly. 'You're so like him, I mean.'

'It's not funny, Dil. I'm scared. I couldn't sleep for thinking about what happened to him. He started drinking and doing dope, you know. Just like me.'

'Yes, well.' She gazed into his troubled face. 'You told me about the dope before. You said it made you ten feet tall and I said look at the kids in the junkie ads – do they look ten feet tall. Remember?'

He nodded. 'You said some rotten things to me, Dil. I went right off you for a while.'

'But I was right, Tim, don't you see? Branwell wanted to be ten feet tall, and look what happened to him.'

Tim nodded. They were going down a tussocky slope, wading through heather. 'I know. I thought about all that for hours, Dil. In bed. I don't need any lectures.

What I want to know is, what do I do? I mean, should I tell somebody I'm a Brontë or what?'

She looked at him. 'You've got to decide for yourself, Tim. You'd be famous.'

'Yes, but I'd be famous because of him, wouldn't I? Not because of me.'

'Right. And anyway they might not believe you. It's not as if there was any actual proof, see? You've got no proof. There'd be loads of art students in London in 1835. It could all be coincidence – even your looking like him. You get lookalikes all the time and they're not related.'

'Right.' He felt a lift. A sense of release. 'So I don't have to do anything, do I?'

Dilys didn't answer. They trudged side by side in the middle of the group, down the slope, across a glacial valley and on to the steep hillside beyond. As they started up, bent under the weight of their gear, Tim saw that Chris and the others had begun to put their plan into operation. They'd crossed the valley floor before the main group was halfway down the slope and now, as Mr Barker led the assault on the hillside, the four of them reached the top and passed from sight. As Chris had predicted, their disappearance caused no concern among the teachers. They were on course, and the group would catch them up when they tired.

As they climbed, a breeze sprang up. It was a light breeze, but cool. It ruffled the new spring grass and wafted soothingly over damp foreheads. Tim inhaled deeply, savouring the refreshing sharpness, the rank, peaty reek of it. The gradient was taking it out of his tired body and he kept looking up. The top seemed close, but it never got noticeably closer.

The breeze was stronger when they finally stood on

the summit, panting and looking back. They seemed to have come miles already. The track they'd crossed in the valley was a thread from here, and Haworth had vanished completely. Behind them and ahead were hills and then more hills, with dark, narrow valleys between. Vegetation was sparse, and there was no sign of human habitation.

The ground immediately before them fell away steeply into a dry, boulder-choked valley in which, here and there, stunted scrub-oaks clung to life. As they started down, dislodging small stones which skittered and bounced in front of them, Tim said, 'I don't believe the Brontës ever did this walk, Dil. How the heck would they manage in those long skirts and button-boots?'

Dilys shrugged. 'Dunno. Maybe they had special gear, like us.'

'Did they hummer! If you ask me, they stick the word Brontë on to anything round here. It doesn't mean a thing.' He grinned. 'Trogging over this lot in ankle-length drawers and a crinoline.'

The valley was difficult and they had to place each foot carefully. A slip here, a turned ankle, and the victim would face a painful journey back. There was no sign of the Barraclough expedition. They'll be halfway up the facing slope by now, thought Tim. Sixpacks and all, but he didn't look. He was too busy watching where he put his feet.

The wind had stiffened. It slammed up the valley, tugged at their packs and pulled a veil of haze across the sun. Tim glanced into the sky and shivered. 'I don't like the look of that, Dil.'

'No. It's not nearly as nice as it was.'

They'd just begun to climb again when Tim looked

back and spotted Chris. He was sitting with his back against a boulder some distance from the track. He had his knees drawn up and his arms wrapped round them. Tim couldn't see the others but he knew they'd be there somewhere – behind the boulder, probably. He looked away quickly, not wanting Dilys to see. He'd promised not to split and he wouldn't, but it was going to be difficult when they got to Wycoller – when the four weren't there and the teachers started panicking. He sighed and climbed doggedly, wishing he'd slept last night. He was halfway up the slope when it started to rain.

# Authentic Brontë Atmosphere

'Hold it a minute, folks.' They had climbed out of the stony valley and were about to follow Mr Barker into the next one, when he raised an arm and Ellis called from the rear.

The party halted, glad of the break. Packs were shrugged off and opened. Kids pulled out kagouls and overtrousers and got into them as the rain fell harder. The teachers conferred, glancing anxiously at the sky. Tim refastened his rucksack and sat on it, trying to eavesdrop, but the wind whipped the words away. He gazed at the hills. Distant ones were milky now, bluish and indistinct. The sodden sky had sunk slowly to earth and sagged now just above his head, propped on hilltops.

'Right, listen.' Kids turned their heads without getting up. Barker and Lidsay walked on. Ellis looked grim.

'The weather's deteriorating rapidly,' he said. 'And in view of the talk we had from the Countryside Warden we've decided to abandon the walk. We're not halfway, so we're going back.'

Groans and boos greeted this announcement and Tariq Ali called out, 'Can't we go on, sir – we've got the proper gear?'

'No, Tariq, I'm afraid we can't. We don't know the terrain ahead, and as I said we're not halfway. Going back will be quicker, and the route more familiar. Mrs Lindsay and Mr Barker have gone to bring back Barraclough and the others. We won't wait for them.'

Tim chewed his lip. Commonsense said he ought to tell Ellis that Lindsay and Barker had gone the wrong way – that Chris and the others were behind, not in front. What if one of the teachers was injured while trying to catch them up? What if they called out the fell rescue guys and sent them in the wrong direction?

He couldn't tell though – he'd promised. And anyway, what was all the panic about? A bit of wind? A drop of rain? It's only four miles back to Haworth, for Pete's sake. It'll work out.

'Come on, then.' Kitted out, the kids straightened up and shouldered their packs. The wind drove rain at their waterproofs with a sound like tearing cloth. Ellis had to shout. 'Take it steady. Stick to the track. Stay behind me.' They set off down the hillside in single file with their heads down. Droplets gathered on Tim's glasses, blinding him. He wiped the lenses with his fingers, half clearing them, thinking, Tiger Tim the spitfire ace never had this problem.

He wanted to ask Dilys what she thought about splitting on Chris. He'd a fair idea what she'd say, though, and anyway she was four places ahead of him so there was no chance. Lindsay and Barker'd be all right. They were grown-up people. They'd be in Wycoller in no time. And it was none of his business, anyway.

Recrossing the valley floor, he thought, this must be where they sloped off. Look: there's a sort of natural pass between the boulders. They went along there and just sat down till we'd gone. That Chris wasn't even bothering to watch us when I looked back, the cheeky sod. Wonder if they're still there?

Surely not. Not in this wind. Not now that it's raining. They'll have packed up and started back to Haworth. They'll be there before us, and they'll tell old Ellis they got lost.

You never know, though. They might have found somewhere dry – a cave or something. After all, the weather wasn't that brilliant when they took off, was it? You could see what was coming but it didn't stop them. They're just about barmy enough to have stayed put, and just about selfish enough not to give a damn who might be risking life and limb looking for them. Think I'll take a look, anyway.

He went down on one knee, fiddling with a bootlace. Two girls trudged by. Jennifer Wilde and Susan Waterhouse. Two down, two to come. A stone rattled. Richard Mayfield swerved round him and rejoined the track. One more.

'Hey up, Timmo,' growled Wilson Hall. 'Don't get left behind.'

'No way.' Tim watched the lad's back till mist and distance dimmed it. 'Don't look round,' he hissed, straightening up.

He left the track and strode between great boulders, following the natural pass. It was raining harder now, and he didn't want to hang about.

He'd travelled about a hundred yards and was about to turn back when he heard voices. He paused, pushing his hood back to listen. There. A laugh. Lee Freeman's silly falsetto laugh away to the right somewhere.

Incredible. He flipped his hood up and moved towards the sound. The mist seemed thicker here, and he was practically on top of the Barraclough Expedition before he saw it.

They were sitting in jeans and sweat-shirts in the lee of a great boulder, under an overhang so deep it was almost a cave. Empty cans and cigarette butts already littered the sandy floor, though they couldn't have been here much longer than half an hour. Tim's unexpected arrival was greeted with tipsy mirth. He ducked into the overhang and squatted, whipping off his glasses. The still air felt warm on his cheeks.

'Anyone got a hanky?' Somebody – he couldn't see who – put one in his hand. 'Thanks.' He polished his lenses, mopped his face, put his glasses on and looked round.

'Why're you still here?' he said. 'Haven't you seen the weather?'

Chris regarded him through half-closed eyes. 'We've seen it, Bran. Here.' He offered an unopened can. 'It's not raining on us, is it?'

Tim shook his head. 'No, thanks. Listen. The walk's off. We all turned back except Lindsay and Barker. They're out there looking for you.'

'More fool them,' chuckled Chris. 'What do you say, fellas?'

'Right.' Janis, cross-legged on the sand, exhaled a

133

plume of smoke. 'They shouldn't have joined if they can't take a joke.'

'They should've done the same as us,' said Lee. 'Found a nice dry cave and got some ale in.' The others laughed.

Tim shook his head. 'Listen. I sneaked off to find you. They'll miss me any minute. We've got to catch them up.'

'Catch them up?' Chris's face wore an amused frown. 'What for, Bran lad? Who'd be daft enough to go out there with all that wuthering going on, when we can sit here safe and dry till it clears?'

'But they're gonna think we're lost, Chris. Injured. They'll get the rescue service out.'

Chris shrugged. 'Up to them. We can't help it if we got lost and had to shelter, can we? The teachers should've been watching us better.'

'You planned it!' retorted Tim. 'You told me.'

'No, we didn't. Not if anybody asks, we didn't. Not if they try to get us done.' He grinned. 'The teachers allowed the party to become strung out over a considerable distance, and four pupils got lost. I can just see it in the *Sun*. "Peril to Pupils in Naff Staff Gaff." They never checked our packs to see if we had the right gear, did they?'

Tim looked at him. 'You wouldn't do that, Chris. Blame old Ellis, I mean.'

'Wouldn't I?' Chris laughed. 'You watch me. And you'd better not stick your two-penn'orth in or I'll fix you and all.'

'Are you saying you haven't any windproof gear with you?'

'Have we heck! How could we have humped all this stuff if we had?'

134

'Well – what you going to do, Chris? It's belting down out there. Blowing a gale. It's cold, and getting colder. It might go on all night.'

'Naw. It'll blow itself out in no time. You go if you want to. We're not.'

'Maybe we should, Chris.' Alvin looked apprehensive. 'Like Timmo said, it might go on all night.'

Chris shot him a scornful glance. 'Go on then, Cooper. Shove off. You've always been chicken, anyway.'

'I'm not chicken. I'm thinking about what that guy said. You can die in a few hours out here.'

'Yeah.' Janis ground her cigarette into the sand and started to get up. 'I think we should go, Chris.'

'Well, you would, wouldn't you? You've got the gear for a start. You've drunk our ale and smoked our ciggies and now you're running out on us.' He looked at Lee. 'You're not yellow as well, are you?' He failed to keep the anxiety out of his voice.

Lee shrugged. ''Course not, Chris, but we did this to get out of the walk, right?'

'So?'

'So the walk's off. We got out of it. We've won, so there's no point staying, is there?'

'No point? What about all this?' He gestured towards the lager and cigarettes. 'Our Phil gave me thirty quid to get this stuff. Thirty quid, and this is the thanks we get. You wait till I tell him, that's all. What a bunch of plonkers!'

Tim's heart kicked. He gazed at the cans and packets. He looked at his friend. He swallowed. 'Thirty pounds? Your Phil's on the dole, Chris. Where'd he get thirty pounds to throw around?'

'What's it to do with you, four-eyes?' growled Chris.

'He came into some readies, right? Maybe he won the pools.'

Sure, thought Tim. And maybe he was listening harder than I thought when I was daft enough to tell him where a certain old lady kept her money. He ducked out of the overhang and straightened. 'I'm off. Who's coming and who's staying?'

Nobody stayed. Chris was sullen, but he wasn't going to stay by himself. He loaded the cigarettes into his pack. He wanted to take the lager too, but Tim told him it was too heavy – dressed as he was, he'd need all his energy.

They rounded the boulder and set off, leaning on the wind. The three ill-clad boys were drenched in seconds. They gasped as the cold struck through the sodden fabric plastered to their limbs. Easy now to see why people die.

Tim found the track. They swung right and began to climb. The wind blew from their left, driving needles of numbing rain into forehead, cheek and ear. Tim set as brisk a pace as he could, aware that his unprotected friends must find shelter as soon as possible. He wiped his sleeve across his glasses and squinted at his watch. They'd been walking twenty minutes. Twenty minutes at three miles an hour equals one mile, near as dammit. One down, three to go.

A few minutes later, wading through a stretch of bog, he realised they were off the track. He stopped and screwed up his eyes, peering into the mist. The others drew level.

'What's up?' gasped Lee through clenched teeth, hugging himself. His shirt was transparent.

'I've lost the track.'

'Well, let's keep going, for God's sake – I'm freezing.'

Tim shook his head. 'Can't just slog on regardless, Lee. We might be going the wrong way. Got to think.'

'You think, then. I'm off.'

'No.' Tim grabbed the boy's sleeve. 'Listen. When we were on the track, the wind was coming from the left, so if we keep it on our left we're bound to be heading the same way, right?'

'Unless there's a bend in the track,' said Janis.

Tim looked at her. 'Trust you!' He knew she had a point, and that he was responsible for the mess they were in. It was he who had talked them into leaving the overhang. They were safe there – dry and warm, and then he'd come along and decided to play the hero. Of course a real hero would've left them there and gone for help wouldn't he, because real heroes use their heads. That warden guy said something about staying put and keeping warm, didn't he, and they could've done it because they had the ideal place. Tim's groan was drowned by the wind.

It was never like this in his fantasies, being a hero. There was always music, for a kickoff, and people watching. Workers in the wheatfields gazed skyward, open-mouthed as he came in on the tail of the Heinkel and opened fire ... waved and cheered as he performed his victory roll ... he could hear those cheers. ... Or like, if he dived into a raging sea to rescue Princess Di or somebody, the jetty lined with holidaymakers ... they'd all be rooting for him ... and then somebody would say something like, bravest damn thing I ever saw.

So start using you head, Tim lad – it isn't too late. 'Listen.' They looked at him. 'Janis and I have kags and also sweaters. I'm giving my sweater to Lee and my

137

overtrousers to Chris. Janis – how about letting Alvin have your sweater?'

'Brilliant,' growled Janis. 'That way we all freeze, instead of just some of us.'

'That way we might all make it.' Tim was already pulling his kag over his head. It snapped and flapped in the wind. He peeled off the thick sweater and handed it to Lee.

'Oh, thanks, Timmo.' Lee pulled it on, and hopped about with clenched teeth to generate some warmth which wouldn't be instantly stripped away by the wind. Janis muttered something unintelligible and surrendered hers to Chris.

'Right. We move fast to get warm, we keep the wind on our left and we stay close together. Let's go.'

They trudged on with their heads down. Tim was more afraid than he had ever been in his life. As he walked, it dawned on him that in real life heroism probably felt like this. There was no cheering in it. No music.

## MISTER IN THE MIST

They'd done about a mile when he saw the man. He crossed their path maybe twenty yards ahead, a shape in the mist.

'Hey! Hey, mister!' Tim plunged forward, waving. The others lifted their heads, saw him too and followed with the strength of sudden hope.

The man neither paused nor turned but strode on,

moving fast. They swerved to match his course but within seconds his outline faded as he outpaced them. Tim, jogging, his eyes locked on the receding figure yelled, 'Don't lose him. Come on!' The temperature was falling and Tim knew that this man, this shepherd or hiker or whatever he was, might easily represent their last chance of reaching safety.

He followed no path that Tim could see, wading through knee-high heather and sphagnum bog with hardly a break in the rhythm of his stride. He seemed to move easily and yet, though Tim and the others almost ran in their desperation, they could not close the gap between themselves and their unwitting guide.

Tim was tiring. There was water in his left boot – icy water which squished every time he laid his foot down. The wind seemed to have strengthened and there was more snow than rain in the sleet. It no longer melted as it hit the ground, but lay like a greyish scum in hollows and on the windward side of stones.

Tim risked a glance behind. Janis was close, and he could see Alvin tucked in behind her, but Chris and Lee had dropped back. The party was becoming strung out as exhaustion set in. He knew he ought to wait but it was impossible. The stranger showed no sign of slackening his pace, and if they lost sight of him they were finished. He stumbled on, gasping, 'Chris. Lee. Close up!' The wind tore the words from his lips and he wasn't sure they'd hear him, or if they'd have the strength to respond if they did. All he could do was keep going and hope it wasn't far now. It couldn't be far now, could it?'

As Tim slogged on, his sense of time started to disintegrate and the idea of finite distances dissolved. There was no destination now, only this howling white infinity through which he was moving, lifting leaden feet and laying them down, first one, then the other. He'd forgotten why he was bothering to keep moving, except that it had something to do with following and being followed. It's silly, really, he thought, because it's not cold anymore and I'm so tired. I could stop for a while and lie down and go to sleep and move on later. Or not move on at all. I could do like – whatsisname. I could say I may be some time and lie down and go to sleep and let it cover me. He giggled. Forever.

'Tim!'

'Huh?' He was lying on something lumpy and his back was cold.

He opened his eyes and saw Janis. Her hood was flapping in the wind. He smiled. 'Hi, Janis. What's up?'

'You fell down, Timmo. You were asleep. We lost the guy.'

'Oh, wow!' He levered himself up on one elbow and shook the fleecy warmth out of his head. Cold wrapped itself around him. He groaned and got up, tottering with weariness. Four pairs of eyes watched him. Frightened eyes.

'Which way'd he go?'

'That way.' Janis pointed. 'I think.'

'Follow, then. It's all we can do.'

Lee shook his head. 'I've had it, Tim.'

'Here, hang about!' Chris was looking down, scuffing the ground with his boot. 'This is a track. We're on a track. A wide one. And look – there's tyre-prints. We're near a farm.'

'Are we heck!' said Lee, brokenly. 'We're miles from anywhere and we're gonna die. I wish I'd never come on this rotten trip.'

Tim looked where Chris was pointing. Those were

140

tyremarks all right. Tractor, by the look of them. They were on a track, and it led downwards. They'd only to follow it down and—.

'We've done it!' he cried. 'We're practically home, Lee. Come on!'

They stumbled on down the track. It was too wide to lose and they made good time. After a while Janis cried, 'Listen!'

'What?'

'A dog. I heard a dog.'

'Terrific. Keep going.'

As they descended, the wind decreased and the sleet turned to rain. The track became rutted with long troughs of sticky yellow clay which sucked at their boots. They didn't care. A rutted track is a well-used track and they were going to make it.

A dog started to bark steadily, and Tim could make out a shadow to his right – a shadow which darkened and solidified till it became a long, low, semi-derelict building. There was an unglazed window with sacking over it and a battered door. They could hear the dog's blunt claws scrabbling at the woodwork. They moved on, and soon there was wan yellow light ahead and a woman's voice calling, 'Hello – are you all right?'

Tim half ran towards the voice. The woman was standing in the middle of the track with floury hands and a butcher's apron. It was as much as Tim could do to keep from flinging his arms round her. 'All right!' he cried. 'We're all right now.' He was laughing and weeping at the same time.

The others came around, grinning and sobbing, and the woman said, 'This way. Quickly, now. Let's get you under cover.'

She led them across a yard and into a stone-flagged

passageway. Warm air, heavy with the fragrance of cooking, enveloped them. At the end of the passage was an open door. They were ushered into a room with a large open hearth on which a fire blazed. There were sofas and armchairs and a long, polished table.

'I'm Brenda,' the woman told them, 'and this is Ponden Hall. Get those wet things off, and I'll be back in a minute.' She noticed Janis. 'You come with me, love.'

They stood by the fire and peeled off their sodden clothes. The thought came to Tim that in ordinary circumstances he'd be deeply embarrassed to undress where a woman could see him. He wouldn't have done it, in fact, but it didn't seem to matter now. Not here. Nothing mattered now, except that it was warm and he wasn't going to die.

'Here.' Brenda came in with thick blankets. 'Wrap yourselves in these and sit down.' She glanced about the room. 'Has your teacher been in here?' They looked at her. 'Teacher?' said Tim.

'Yes. The man you're with. Isn't he your teacher?'

'We're not with a man.'

'But he—.' She looked at Tim. 'He knocked. Said you were coming. That's why I was out there looking for you.'

'Ah.' Tim's face cleared. 'We followed a guy. He didn't wait or look back, even when we shouted. We thought he hadn't seen us but he must have.'

Brenda nodded. 'Was he a short, red-headed man with a big nose and glasses, wearing a cape?'

Tim shrugged under the blanket. 'Dunno. We never got near. He was just a shape in the—.' He stopped. 'What did you say he was like?'

Brenda looked at him. 'Short. Five foot or five one. Long red hair. Why?'

'Glasses?'

'That's right.'

'And a cape – you said he was wearing a cape?'

'Yes. It struck me as a bit odd, to tell you the truth.' She frowned. 'Are you feeling all right, love? You've gone very pale.'

'Yeah.' Tim nodded. 'I'm okay, thanks.' He didn't feel okay but he didn't want her to start asking questions. 'Would you call the hostel and tell 'em we're here? They'll be looking for us.'

'Of course. Longlands, is it?'

'Yes.'

'I'll do it now. Wish I knew who that man was, though.' She went out.

Tim sat, clutching the blanket and gazing into the fire. He was warmer now but he couldn't control the shivering. He knew who the man was. Oh yes. He knew exactly who he was, only he mustn't tell anybody else. Not ever. He pulled the blanket more snugly round his throat and gazed into the flames.

\*

Janis rejoined them, dressed in borrowed things. Brenda brought hot drinks and took their clothes away to be dried. Later she brought food and talked quietly with them as they ate. The wind, cheated of its prey, racketed about the walls and roared down the chimney and flung rain at the window.

Presently they heard a horn outside and it was Dawn from the hostel with her Range-Rover. Dressed in blankets and borrowed footwear they trooped along the passageway and into the vehicle. Old Ellis was there. Tim thought he'd be hopping mad, but he smiled and seemed pleased to see them. They waved and shouted thanks to Brenda, and then clung on to anything they could find as the vehicle bounced and jolted down the track.

# A Fragment Will Persist

I am back. Nobody knows why. Nobody shall.

By day I keep to my room, seeing no one. At dusk, as befits a species of rodent, I scurry forth seeking sustenance which, when I have found it, I carry back in bottles to my lair.

It gives me dreams. To dream is not the same as to hope, but dreams dull the pain of hopelessness. Sometimes, too, a fragment will persist, giving rise to hope. Such a dream was mine last night.

It was a cold dream. A white dream. I was walking, head bowed and half blind in the teeth of a wind which keened like a mourner and cut me to the bone. It was years from now, I think. I was making toward a place of safety and, though I did not see them, I knew there followed in my footsteps those whose very lives depended on my lead. I believe they were my children.

I awoke before the thing resolved itself, yet the fragment does not fade. It is a sign, whose meaning is this: that in spite of all its vicissitudes, my life is destined to stand as an example of what a man might accomplish if he dares to dream.

So much for those who say that I am mad.

# WORLD WAR THREE

Old Ellis made them go to bed. A doctor came. He said they just needed sleep and left pills. The other three boys were sleeping now, but Tim didn't take his straight away. Incredibly, it was only six o'clock. He lay listening to the rain on the window. The wind in the trees.

Ellis had been up to see him. Well done, young South, he'd said. Saved your friends' lives, y'know. He wished it were true, but it wasn't. He'd got them all lost and been dead scared and they'd be out there now if it hadn't been for . . .

He couldn't tell anyone. They'd think he was crazy. He could just imagine it. We followed a guy, only he wasn't a living person – he was a ghost. Why sure he was, son. Put this strait-jacket on and come with us.

And then there's this other thing. This Brontë business. He lay with his hands behind his head, gazing at the ceiling. I don't want to tell anybody about that. Like Dil says, there's no proof, and anyway what'd happen if they believed me? I'd be a sort of walking exhibit, wouldn't I? I'd get letters from loonies and make a complete wassock of myself on chat shows. They'd ask me stuff about the Brontës, as if I was an expert or something. I'd probably end up having to swot up on *Wuthering Heights* and *Villette* and about six million poems so I could answer their stupid questions, and it's taking me all my time to get through *Jane Eyre*.

No. I'll probably never be famous but if I am, it'll be because of who I am, not because of who he was. I'm going to keep quiet, and ask Dil to do the same.

\*

It was nearly seven when Dilys came. He smiled. 'I knew you'd come.'

'How you feeling, Tim?'

'Okay, I guess.'

'You should be proud.' She nodded towards the three sleepers. 'They're here because of you.'

He shrugged in the sleeping bag. 'I didn't really do anything, Dil. How's Janis?'

'She's asleep. They're in bother, though. Janis says they got lost, but Ellis isn't daft. She still smells like a brewery and Barraclough's pack was full of fags.'

'What about Lindsay and Barker?'

'They trekked all the way to Wycoller, then raised the alarm.' She laughed. 'It was panic stations around here for a bit, I can tell you. First the Barraclough gang, then you. Nobody missed you till we were back in Haworth, y'know. We thought you were at the back somewhere. There were coppers running all over the place yelling into radios, phones ringing, folk dashing about. World war three wasn't in it.'

'But it's all come out okay, hasn't it?'

'Sure. Listen, love. I'd better go. I'm out of bounds here.'

She bent swiftly, kissed him on the forehead and fled with flaming cheeks.

# AND THEN THERE'S ME

Tim was home by three on Friday, fit as a butcher's dog. His mum was pleased to see him.

'Did you have a nice time?'

'Yes, thank you, Mum. Is Grandma all right?'

'Yes. She went home yesterday.' She gave him a funny look. 'They caught the chap who broke into her flat, Tim. You'd never guess who it was.'

Oh, yes, I would, he thought, but he said, 'Who?'

'It was that Phillip Barraclough. You know – Christopher's brother.'

Surprise, surprise. 'Is he in prison, then?'

'He's out on bail, but I expect he'll go to prison. He had drugs on him.' She smiled sadly. 'Not a very happy homecoming for your friend Chris, Tim.'

He shook his head. 'No.'

He carried his stuff up to his room, unpacked and took the rucksack and empty case to the attic. He took the portrait up there, too. He looked at it under the skylight.

'Maybe your life didn't amount to much,' he murmured. 'Not at the time. But it wasn't for nothing. No way. There's Becky for a kickoff, up there in Edinburgh. She's going to be a doctor, y'know. And then there's me.' He smiled. 'My life hasn't amounted to much so far, but watch me, okay? Keep watching.' He dropped the picture in a boxful of junk and went downstairs.

His dad came in at five. Tim was squatting over a sheet of newspaper on the kitchen floor, scraping mud off his boots.

'Hello, Tim. How was Haworth?'

'Okay, thanks.'

'Did you learn anything?'

Tim smiled wanly. 'I learned something.'

'Good. Heard about young Barraclough, have you?'

'Yes.' He straightened up. 'Mum told me.'

'Picked up Tuesday evening. Too damn late of course – your grandma's money's gone.'

'Not all of it, Dad,' said Tim quietly. 'Not quite.' He felt in his pocket. 'There's fifteen pounds of it here.' He laid the crumpled notes on the table. His father looked at the money, then at his son.

'What the devil d'you mean, Tim? That can't be your grandma's money, surely? Where did you find it?'

'I didn't find it, Dad. Not exactly.'

'Then how? I mean—.'

'I—.' He faltered. He'd meant to tell the truth but it was their eyes. He couldn't stand their eyes. The expressions in them. The way they looked at him.

There's this new teacher at school, see. Dow Jones. Bit of a tycoon. Plays the stock market, and he says to me, if you can get hold of a few quid quickly—.

No! He screwed up his face and shook his head. The fantasy disintegrated. He looked straight at his father.

'I stole it, Dad,' he said.

# READ MORE IN PUFFIN

For children of all ages, Puffin represents quality and variety – the very best in publishing today around the world.

For complete information about books available from Puffin – and Penguin – and how to order them, contact us at the appropriate address below. Please note that for copyright reasons the selection of books varies from country to country.

**On the worldwide web**: www.puffin.co.uk

**In the United Kingdom**: Please write to *Dept. EP, Penguin Books Ltd, Bath Road, Harmondsworth, West Drayton, Middlesex UB7 ODA*

**In the United States**: Please write to *Consumer Sales, Penguin USA, P.O. Box 999, Dept. 17109, Bergenfield, New Jersey 07621-0120*. VISA and MasterCard holders call 1-800-253-6476 to order Penguin titles

**In Canada**: Please write to *Penguin Books Canada Ltd, 10 Alcorn Avenue, Suite 300, Toronto, Ontario M4V 3B2*

**In Australia**: Please write to *Penguin Books Australia Ltd, P.O. Box 257, Ringwood, Victoria 3134*

**In New Zealand**: Please write to *Penguin Books (NZ) Ltd, Private Bag 102902, North Shore Mail Centre, Auckland 10*

**In India**: Please write to *Penguin Books India Pvt Ltd, 706 Eros Apartments, 56 Nehru Place, New Delhi 110 019*

**In the Netherlands**: Please write to *Penguin Books Netherlands bv, Postbus 3507, NL-1001 AH Amsterdam*

**In Germany**: Please write to *Penguin Books Deutschland GmbH, Metzlerstrasse 26, 60594 Frankfurt am Main*

**In Spain**: Please write to *Penguin Books S. A., Bravo Murillo 19, 1° B, 28015 Madrid*

**In Italy**: Please write to *Penguin Italia s.r.l., Via Felice Casati 20, I–20124 Milano*

**In France**: Please write to *Penguin France S. A., 17 rue Lejeune, F–31000 Toulouse*

**In Japan**: Please write to *Penguin Books Japan, Ishikiribashi Building, 2–5–4, Suido, Bunkyo-ku, Tokyo 112*

**In South Africa**: Please write to *Longman Penguin Southern Africa (Pty) Ltd, Private Bag X08, Bertsham 2013*